ALSO BY
Melissa Glenn Haber

The Heroic Adventure of Hercules Amsterdam

Beyond the Dragon Portal

Beyond the Dragon Portal

MELISSA GLENN HABER

DUTTON CHILDREN'S BOOKS

DUTTON CHILDREN'S BOOKS
A division of Penguin Young Readers Group

Published by the Penguin Group
Penguin Group (USA) Inc., 375 Hudson Street, New York, New York 10014, U.S.A.
Penguin Group (Canada), 90 Eglinton Avenue East, Suite 700, Toronto, Ontario, Canada
M4P 2Y3 (a division of Pearson Penguin Canada Inc.) • Penguin Books Ltd, 80 Strand, London
WC2R 0RL, England • Penguin Ireland, 25 St Stephen's Green, Dublin 2, Ireland
(a division of Penguin Books Ltd) • Penguin Group (Australia), 250 Camberwell Road,
Camberwell, Victoria 3124, Australia (a division of Pearson Australia Group Pty Ltd)
Penguin Books India Pvt Ltd, 11 Community Centre, Panchsheel Park, New Delhi - 110 017, India
Penguin Group (NZ), Cnr Airborne and Rosedale Roads, Albany, Auckland 1310, New Zealand
(a division of Pearson New Zealand Ltd) • Penguin Books (South Africa) (Pty) Ltd,
24 Sturdee Avenue, Rosebank, Johannesburg 2196, South Africa • Penguin Books Ltd,
Registered Offices: 80 Strand, London WC2R 0RL, England

Library of Congress Cataloging-in-Publication Data

Haber, Melissa Glenn, date.
Beyond the dragon portal / by Melissa Glenn Haber.—1st ed.   p. cm.
Summary: When her younger sister disappears into a land of dragons and
other strange creatures, eleven-year-old Sadie travels through a portal
to rescue her with the aid of Mrs. Fitz Edna, a most unusual babysitter.
ISBN 0-525-47537-0
[1. Sisters—Fiction. 2. Dragons—Fiction. 3. Babysitters—Fiction.
4. Magic—Fiction. 5. Fantasy.] I. Title.
PZ7.H111335Bey 2005   [Fic]—dc22   2005002368

Published in the United States by
Dutton Children's Books, a division of Penguin Young Readers Group
345 Hudson Street, New York, New York 10014
www.penguin.com/youngreaders

Designed by Beth Herzog

Printed in USA   First Edition
1 3 5 7 9 10 8 6 4 2

Support for this book was provided by:

My husband, Ezra Glenn

My editor, Lucia Monfried

Her assistant, Sarah Pope

My agent, Erin Murphy

. . . and by comments and encouragement from:

Bob Edwards, Jim Haber, Lydia Lake, Susan Larson,

Deborah Haber, Linus Glenhaber, Tobit Glenhaber,

All my in-laws, Sarah Bennett-Astesano, Jennifer Berger,

Jennifer Costa, Anna Guillemin, Kate Horsley,

The Nicely-Johnsons, Eliza Lake, Tonia Prescott,

Rebecca Rabinowitz, Ben Steinberg, Robert Wexelblatt,

Esther Binstock, and Zoe Blickenderfer

and most especially

Mehitabel Glenhaber,

who first told me about Dragonland
and to whom this book is most affectionately
DEDICATED
(although she assures me I got it all wrong).

Contents

Beyond the
Dragon Portal

1

The Normal Day

It all seemed so normal that last day, that day before Sadie Ann Guthrie's life changed forever. The summer sunshine was pouring through the windows and splashing into the comfortable chaos of the kitchen; the oatmeal boiled on the stove; the coffeepot hissed on the counter; and Sadie's little sister, Phoebe, was going on and on about her trip to Dragonland the night before. No one paid too much attention. Their father ran into the kitchen, swore mildly that he'd forgotten to shave, and dashed out again. Their mother stood next to the stove, writing invisible checklists in the air and forgetting to stir the oatmeal. She kept up a one-sided monologue of pleasantries that occasionally coincided with Phoebe's narrative, answering her daughter's tale with a "huh," or a "hmm," or a "that's nice," paying no more attention to the story than she did to the oatmeal, which was beginning to burn. Sadie herself was reading from a battered paperback and ignoring her sister completely. It wasn't like she hadn't heard it all before, anyway. Her sister had been telling the same story since she was three years old.

"The Dragons were late to pick me up last night," Phoebe was saying now. "They had a new basket that hung between them, and it was swinging when they carried me to Dragonland."

"That's nice," their mother said. Sadie rolled her eyes behind her book as her sister droned on about the meadows of moongrass and how she wove garlands of starflowers while the grandfather unicorn told her stories. Even if she hadn't heard Phoebe's story a billion times before, it wasn't the kind of thing to keep Sadie's interest—she didn't have much patience with fantasies. As she had often told her parents, the world was so very full of real problems that she didn't have time for made-up ones. Sadie concentrated so hard on the world's real problems that her father always said she was indefatigable. Sadie knew a lot about the world's troubles but not what *indefatigable* meant. Her father said it meant all her energy made him tired.

"On the way back last night, the Dragons took me past a castle," Phoebe plowed on. "It was all made out of glass."

"That's nice," replied their mother absently, making a mark on the invisible checklist in the air.

This time the one-sided monologue of pleasantries didn't work.

"*No,*" said Phoebe, fixing her odd goldish eyes on their mother as she shook her head vehemently. "It wasn't nice at *all*. It was made out of black glass and there weren't any windows and the Dragons said bad people lived there."

Sadie looked up briefly at this new installment of the story before returning to her book.

"There was a light in the castle," Phoebe went on. "A red light."

"Sounds exciting," said their mother.

"The Dragons were *scared,*" Phoebe persisted. "I've never seen them scared before. The red light kept turning round the top of the castle, and the Dragons didn't want to fly into it."

"That's nice."

"I wonder what they were scared of?" Phoebe pressed.

"Mom!" Sadie shouted, wrinkling her nose. "The oatmeal's burning!"

"Huh? Oh, thank you, Sadie." Their mother looked down at the smoking oatmeal. "I'm sorry, kids—I'm just so distracted. And I wanted to make you a nice breakfast before we left you for the weekend!" Her eyes flew up to the clock. "Oh, where *is* Mrs. Fitz Edna?" she asked in agitation. "If she doesn't come soon, we're going to miss our plane."

Sadie looked from her book to her mother and decided reading was less interesting than getting to be the one in charge. "You can go, you know," she said proudly. "I can watch Phoebe until Mrs. Fitz Edna gets here. I *am* eleven, you know. And I'm very dependable."

Sadie's mother hesitated. She looked from the clock to Sadie's father, who stood next to their suitcase in the doorway, tapping the face of his watch. At last she relented. She gave Sadie a grateful smile and a quick hug before kissing Phoebe on the head. "Tell the Dragons to take care of you while I'm gone," she said, and then she ran out of the kitchen, wiping her hands on her pants and calling out to her husband to start the car.

Competently, dependably, Sadie put the blackened oatmeal pan into the sink for Mrs. Fitz Edna to deal with later. She helped her parents out the door and returned to the kitchen to find Phoebe sampling a morsel of burnt oatmeal from the edge of the pan. Sadie smiled at her charge, but then she remembered something. Darting back through the house, she stopped her parents just as they were about to turn out of the driveway.

"Wait!" she called.

Her father rolled down the window. "What is it, Sades? Is it Phoebe?"

"I just forgot to say 'Be safe.'" That's what they always said in their family, anytime someone left the house: *Be safe.* If anybody ever forgot, Sadie felt sick all day.

"You be safe, too," her father said, smiling.

"Of course *I'll* be safe," said Sadie darkly. "*I'm* not the one going on an airplane."

"Well, you know what they say," their father joked, putting the car back into reverse, "ninety percent of accidents happen within two miles of the home. Fifty percent of them probably occur right in the house—twenty percent, at least, in the bathtub."

He was making fun of the way she used statistics. Sadie made a face at him. "Accidents don't happen to *me*," she said. "*I'm* very careful."

"Well, make sure they don't happen to Phoebe, then," her father said, giving her a wink.

"I love you, Sadie," called her mother from the passenger seat. "See you Monday night, all right?"

"Right. Be safe."

"Be safe."

"Bye."

Sadie stood on the front steps, watching them pull away, and then she went back into the house.

Mrs. Fitz Edna was sitting at the kitchen table next to Phoebe when Sadie returned. "I let myself in the back door," she explained in her comforting, growly voice. "Your sister was just telling me about her trip to Dragonland last night." She drew on her cigarette, and two elegant plumes of smoke poured out of her nose. Mrs. Fitz Edna was always smoking. Despite Sadie's indefatigable efforts to make her stop, she always had a cigarette in at least one of her hands. Sadie's mother always said she would have fired any other baby-sitter who insisted on smoking, but Mrs. Fitz Edna was clearly irreplaceable—no one else would have listened to Phoebe's interminable Dragonland stories with such pretended interest.

"Yes, indeed," she mused now, "this news is disturbing, quite disturbing indeed. I must say, Princess, I much prefer it when you tell me you went to the meadows of starflowers." A smoky beard rolled out of her mouth, and then, as if coming out of her reverie, she leapt to her feet.

"But what am I doing, letting the grass grow under my feet! I should be making breakfast for you poor little chicks! What shall it be, then? Poached eggs on toast? Pancakes with fruit? Speak, my hatchlings, your Mrs. Fitz Edna is here to serve."

Despite her disappointment at not getting to be the dependable one in charge, Sadie smiled and curled her toes in anticipation of Mrs. Fitz Edna's delicious breakfast. She loved Mrs. Fitz Edna. Her mother always said that their babysitter was decidedly strange, but Sadie thought she was decidedly delightful. It was true that she was very funny-looking, with her extraordinarily large behind that seemed to push her forward at the waist, and it was certainly true that she stank of cigarettes, but to Sadie she was like a second mother. Phoebe, too, adored her. Now the little girl was nestled up close to Mrs. Fitz Edna at the kitchen counter and staring up lovingly as their babysitter whipped up the pancakes. She cracked an egg deftly with one hand as she held the cigarette in the other, and smiled down on the little girl beside her. She adored Phoebe. In the five years since she had moved next door, there had not been a moment she had not treated Phoebe like a princess. Sadie she treated like a knight in shining armor.

That was perhaps what Sadie liked best about Mrs. Fitz Edna. When other grown-ups laughed at Sadie for her earnestness, or made light of her serious attempts to improve the world, Mrs. Fitz Edna was always there to encourage her in her convictions. She never made fun of Sadie by calling her *indefatigable*. Instead, she praised Sadie for her commitment.

"You have three great qualities," she'd told Sadie once. "And those qualities are your loyalty, your courage, and your great sense of outrage. And I will tell you this: these are all qualities we will come to count on in the coming days."

Now Sadie smiled at Mrs. Fitz Edna over her pancakes and wrinkled her nose with contentment.

"So, Sadie," Mrs. Fitz Edna began, cigarette smoke billowing from her mouth, "I assume you already have plans for the day? Will you be making hay while the sun shines?"

"I'm going to see my friend Picker."

"Ah, yes: the boy with the untamable cowlick." She blew out a great quantity of blue smoke through her nose. "That seems an admirable occupation for the day. And you, Princess Phoebe, have you given thought to what we shall do?"

"I want you to tell me a Dragon story. I want the story of Sigurd and Fafner."

"A fine story—a taste of Dragon blood that can make you talk to the animals. Very well, Princess, let us go up and get you dressed, and I will tell you the story. And then, perhaps, you will tell me more of the news of Dragonland. Don't worry about the dishes, Sadie. I will do them later."

Sadie had been moving towards the sink at a very languid pace, hoping Mrs. Fitz Edna would make just that offer. Willingly, she left her plate on the counter, shoved the paperback from the table into the back pocket of her cutoff jeans, and went to find Picker.

She found him in his garage, head bent over something, one blond cowlick curling up towards the ceiling. He looked up happily when she came through the open door.

"Sadie!" he said, holding out something. "I found the totally perfect control panel for the robot we're going to make!"

"I didn't know we were going to make a robot," Sadie answered, examining the panel of little switches that might have once belonged to a La-Z-Boy recliner, labeled HEAD, FEET, SEAT, ARMS.

"Well, obviously we couldn't, until I found *this*. You can't make a robot before you have the control panel—it might run totally amok. What would we do if it started moving and we couldn't control its seat?"

Sadie acceded to the wisdom of this statement, and they spent the morning fashioning the robot out of whatever spare bits of wire and metal they could find in the garage. It was not yet done when Picker sat back on his heels and rubbed the sweaty cowlick out his eyes.

"You know what?" he said.

"It's too hot?"

"Yeah. You know what we should do?"

"The quarry? That's just what I was thinking. Let's go swimming."

It was just past one, and the old quarry was full of kids. There was an enormous wait to ride on the rope that would swing you out over the water, and all the good flat places on the rocks were taken up by girls sunbathing in their little bikinis. Sadie and Picker dove under the waters, finally coming up, lungs bursting, next to the trailing willow fronds on the far side of the quarry. Picker's cowlick was plastered down on top of his head. He looked very odd without it.

"You know what I want to do?" he asked.

"Let's see—is it what you want to do every day?"

"Yes."

"It's too dangerous."

"Where's your sense of adventure?"

"I don't need a sense of adventure. There's nothing there."

There was a legend in their town that halfway down the quarry's marble walls, deep under the green water, there was a dark passageway that led somewhere mysterious. Some said that was why the quarry was abandoned and allowed to fill in with rain; others, like Sadie, said it was all garbage. She repeated that now before spitting out a long and elegant fountain of quarry water between her teeth.

"But what if it's *not* garbage?" Picker challenged. "What if there's something totally excellent down there? Maybe it leads somewhere exciting."

"Even if it did, we'd drown before we got there."

"We could send down the robot," Picker suggested.

"Okay," said Sadie, trying to climb up a fistful of willow branches. "If we ever finish it."

They swam for an hour, one looking for the cave and one not looking, before they waited the interminable wait for their turn to fling themselves over the water on the rope swing. Finally, as the summer sun dragged itself slowly into the west, they lay side by side on the hot rocks and read aloud the works of Mr. George Orwell from the damp paperback in Sadie's back pocket. It was, Sadie determined, a decidedly perfect day.

She was still thinking about it later that night in bed when she heard the knock on her bedroom door. It was Phoebe.

"What is it?" Sadie asked, a little annoyed at being disturbed.

"You didn't say it," Phoebe complained in a hurt voice. "You didn't say 'be safe' when I went to bed."

"I don't say 'be safe' when people go to bed—I say it when they leave the house."

"Say it now!"

"All right, all right, *be safe*—how's that? Now leave me alone. I want to go to sleep."

Phoebe didn't say anything. She could be an intense little child, and she looked intense now. Her gold-colored eyes were very serious, and she was breathing heavily through her open mouth.

"Jeez, Phoebe, move back! It's boiling enough without getting your hot breath all over me!"

Phoebe continued to stare, her hunched shoulders drawn up even more than usual.

Sadie sighed. "What is it?" she asked, rolling her eyes. Then she remembered she had promised her parents to take care of her sister, and she started over in a nicer voice. "Do you want to sleep here, with me?"

"I *can't* sleep in here," Phoebe objected in that exasperatingly stubborn way of hers. "The Dragons won't know where to find me."

"Well, what do you *want*, then? You should be asleep already."

Phoebe pouted a little. Then she said sadly: "Good night, Sadie. Be safe."

"Be safe," repeated Sadie, turning her attention back to her book. "Come on now, I said it. Go back to bed."

Without waiting for Phoebe to leave, Sadie rolled over and pulled the sheet up to her neck. In a moment the book slipped out of her hand, and she began to slide into sleep. The fan made a reassuring buzzing sound, the sheets were smooth and cool, and Sadie felt decidedly comfortable. She heard Mrs. Fitz Edna wheezing in the hall, and that, too, was a normal, familiar sound.

But when she woke up in the morning, the sounds coming from the hall were not normal at all. Mrs. Fitz Edna was standing at Phoebe's door and crying as if her heart would break.

"What is it? What is it?" Sadie cried, leaping out of bed. Mrs. Fitz Edna turned to her with a look of uncontrolled misery. Both hands pulled at her hair and twisted her clothes, and the tears ran down her wrinkled cheeks.

"The Princess is gone!" she wailed. "They didn't bring her home!" Sadie stared. Great plumes of smoke were pouring from Mrs. Fitz Edna's nose and mouth. There was nothing strange about that, of course—except that there was no cigarette to be seen anywhere about her.

2

≈

The Not-Normal Day

In books, people often respond to strange events by pinching themselves and wondering if they are in a dream, but that is not what happened to Sadie. She stood there in the middle of Phoebe's empty room, watching Mrs. Fitz Edna wail, and she knew with a sinking feeling that she was wide awake. She was not in a dream, and Mrs. Fitz Edna had clearly gone crazy.

"Mrs. Fitz Edna?" she started tentatively. "Would you like a cup of tea?" But Mrs. Fitz Edna only wept harder. She was looking very disheveled. Her gray cardigan was buttoned crookedly, and one of her feet was covered with a slipper and the other by a tall gum boot that belonged to Sadie's father. Her long coils of gray hair were coming down even more than usual, and they made her look very strange. But worst of all was the inexplicable blue smoke that continued to pour out of her.

It was very upsetting to see a grown-up in this state, and Sadie wanted to stamp her feet and demand that Mrs. Fitz Edna act her age.

"Phoebe *can't* be gone, Mrs. Fitz Edna," she insisted. "She probably just went downstairs to get some cereal. She does that sometimes, you know. She thinks she's all grown up, now that she's five. Please, *please,* Mrs. Fitz Edna! Don't cry like that! Let's go downstairs and get Phoebe!"

But Mrs. Fitz Edna seemed incapable of doing anything but weeping, and the smoke poured from her nose and mouth in great rolling waves like the ghosts of words she could not say. This distressed Sadie even further.

"Mrs. Fitz Edna!" she screamed. "Either stop all that smoke or . . . light a cigarette!"

Mrs. Fitz Edna looked down at the great apron of smoke that was rolling down her chest, and she sat down heavily on Phoebe's floor.

"I forgot," she said. "The shock of it . . . well, now you know."

"Now I *know?*" Sadie repeated stupidly. "Now I know what? I have no idea what you're talking about!"

"I think you do," said Mrs. Fitz Edna. "You're a very smart girl."

Sadie stared at the blue smoke, and sniffed: it was not the

disgusting stale smell of tobacco, but something older—the smell of old eggs, maybe, or sulfur, which used to be called brimstone. And then, just in the way she knew that everything that was happening was not a dream, Sadie knew what Mrs. Fitz Edna was trying to tell her. Without saying another word, she ran down the stairs, calling Phoebe's name, screaming Phoebe's name, shrieking Phoebe's name, but there was no Phoebe in the house at all, except in the echoes of her name as Sadie called again and again for the little sister who was not there.

At last she returned to Phoebe's bedroom. Mrs. Fitz Edna was beyond tears now, though the smoke still cascaded down her chest in great miserable curls.

"I suppose you're sure she didn't leave the house by herself," asked Sadie.

"I slept in front of her door," Mrs. Fitz Edna confirmed. "Just to be certain, I slept there, on the floor. She did not leave her room last night if she did not leave by the window."

Phoebe's blue curtains flapped lazily in the breeze. Sadie stuck her head out the window and looked: there was a three-story drop to the ground outside.

"She really went to Dragonland, then?" Sadie asked, not really believing it, but at the same time knowing for certain that it was so.

Mrs. Fitz Edna nodded miserably. Smoke continued to pour out of her nose and throat like a lamentation.

"And you—you're a Dragon, aren't you?"

An imperceptible nod.

Sadie sighed. Her legs felt very weak. There was only one thing to do.

"I've got to call my parents. . . ." she said, heading for the door, but Mrs. Fitz Edna grasped her by the hand.

"Don't you understand?" she whispered desperately, holding Sadie's hand very tightly. "My grief is self-indulgent, but as they say, time and tide wait for no man. We must go *now*, Sadie Ann. We must go rescue Phoebe."

Sadie could only stare.

"We?" she repeated. "Me? *I* can't go rescue her. . . ."

"You must," Mrs. Fitz Edna insisted. "There is no choice." The smoke flowed out of her in great curlicues now, and the gray hair had come entirely down.

"But I'm only eleven."

"Irrelevant," Mrs. Fitz Edna snorted. "Your parents are only forty: you are all infants. We must go."

Sadie began to object further, but Mrs. Fitz Edna had clearly made up her mind. Before Sadie's incredulous eyes, she began to change. Her thick legs grew thicker, and stouter, and then her arms began to shrink. From beneath the broad tweed skirt, always held at an awkward angle by her enormous behind, came a long, uncurling tail; the hump beneath the cardigan hunched even more and then stretched, revealing a long and serpentine neck, and her face grew broader and flatter, somewhat like the noble face of a lion. Then the Dragon who had once been Mrs. Fitz Edna hit the ground on all fours, twelve feet from tooth to tail. Sadie closed her eyes. *This is decidedly unbelievable,* she thought. *Maybe it's just as well I'm the only one here. I think it would pretty much kill my parents to see what I've just seen.*

"We must leave now," croaked the Dragon who had been Mrs. Fitz Edna. "I never thought I would allow a creature, much less a human, to crawl upon my back, but these are desperate times. . . . I have no basket to carry you, but necessity is the mother of invention, as they say. Let's see—get the garden hose from the garage. That should do it, if you can't find any rope."

"I need to write a note to my parents, too," said Sadie in a daze. "I don't want them to worry more than they need to."

Wishing that it would all turn out to be a dream after all, Sadie collected the hose and tied on her sneakers before going to the kitchen to write a note. The sun was coming through the windows and splashing onto the kitchen table just like any other morning, but this was decidedly not like any other day. Sadie stood for a moment over the blank piece of paper, wondering what to say, before scribbling out a few reassuring words. At last she tacked the paper to the front door so her parents would not have to look for it, and then she climbed back up the stairs to Phoebe's room.

The Dragon who had once been Mrs. Fitz Edna was pacing back and forth on the blue carpet, coughing in a rhythmic sort of way. Great streams of smoke shot from her mouth, and Sadie suddenly felt very nervous.

"Do you have to do that?" she asked.

"Of course I have to do that," the Dragon Fitz Edna replied. "How do you expect me to fly without a system for propulsion?"

"Fly?" repeated Sadie weakly. "We have to *fly* to Dragonland? I thought, because you don't have any wings . . ."

"Wings!" scoffed the Dragon in Mrs. Fitz Edna's voice, in the same tone she used whenever Phoebe suggested they eat at McDonald's. "*Wings* are for grebes and pigeons. My People fly without wings—we shoot out smoke and steam to move us forward, an idea copied by your jets and rockets, not to mention your squid and octopus. Come, Sadie. You know what is at stake."

With a sigh meant to settle the pounding of her heart in her throat, Sadie looked at the Dragon's scaly back. She felt the same way she did whenever it was her turn to jump from the rope swing into the quarry: a mix of bravery and daredevilry and the feeling that the only way to confront your fears was to act so quickly you could not stop yourself. She climbed aboard the Dragon, feeling the smooth hard scales like the shell of a turtle through the thin material of her summer pajamas. She tied the hose around her waist and then around the Dragon's neck in a series of figure eights, topping the whole thing off with a collection of complicated knots. She did it reluctantly, without enthusiasm, and the whole time she was thinking, *This is it. This is the moment I am growing up: I am doing something I would give anything not to do just because I'm the only one who can. And I promised. I promised I would take care of Phoebe.*

"Are you ready?" the Dragon growled, coughing out a puff of smoke.

"No," said Sadie, "I'm not."

"Nonsense," grunted the Dragon, and in her voice, Sadie heard an echo of Mrs. Fitz Edna the day she'd insisted Sadie lose her training wheels. *Nonsense!* Mrs. Fitz Edna had said. *Of course you can do it. Don't use a crutch if you can walk, Sadie Ann Guthrie.* Strangely, it made her feel braver.

The Dragon seemed to sense the change in Sadie, and her long body seemed to relax a little. She walked a few steps forwards and to the side as if to settle the weight on her back, and brusquely inquired if Sadie needed a pillow to improve the comfort of her seat. Then, awkwardly (or perhaps arthritically, if Dragons could have arthritis), she turned herself around.

"Watch out—" Sadie warned as the long serpentine tail swung into Phoebe's dollhouse, scattering the little dolls and their possessions all over the floor. The Dragon who had so recently been Mrs. Fitz Edna backed up to the window, wiggling her tail and hind legs out onto the sill. Sadie had the briefest glimpse of Phoebe's dolls lying surprised on their backs, staring up at the ceiling, and then the Dragon Fitz Edna let out an enormous bellow of smoke and steam that shot them right out the window. Phoebe's room was gone: they were outside in the sunshine of a new June day, with the Dragon's tail pointing towards the sky and Sadie's face pointing straight down towards the deserted street. It was not at all how people rode on Dragons in books.

"Hey!" she called out, in panic, staring down at the deserted street. "Hey! We're upside down!"

The Dragon blew out another great gust of smoke that shot them upwards, as if to indicate she was too busy to explain, and Sadie understood that it was the hot air the Dragon blew out of her mouth that was pushing them upwards. If she hadn't wanted to be upside down for their upwards journey, she realized, she should have sat facing the Dragon's tail. She sighed again, deeply, but the Dragon had no time for regrets. She flew around the house once, twice, to get up speed, and then they were off, leaving no signs of their departure but the hastily scrawled note on the door:

Mom, Dad —
Don't worry — I've gone off to rescue Phoebe.
Tell Picker I'm sorry I won't be there to help
with the robot.
BACK SOON.
Love, Sadie
P.S. I hope your trip to California was good.

3

Dragonland

Sadie held on for dear life. The ground below grew smaller and smaller, first less like her neighborhood and more like a map, and then less like a map and more like a splotchy picture of blue and green and brown. Everything felt wrong: her blood was in her head and her heart was in her throat, and she gripped the Dragon's scaly sides with both arms and legs. Riding on Mrs. Dragon Edna (or was it Mrs. Fitz Dragon?) was like riding an eel through water. The Dragon twisted in the air, twining and turning to catch the best currents in the wind, and Sadie was too dizzy to think.

They rose higher and higher through the cooling air, sometimes passing through damp and wispy clouds that soaked Sadie's thin pajamas. The only sound from the Dragon was the bellows sigh of her breath and great exhalations of smoke, and as Sadie slowly stopped worrying she would fall, she began to feel a terrible loneliness pressing against her like the cold. She wished her parents were there. More than once she wished for Picker, who would have thrilled to the idea of shooting straight into the sky on the back of a long and snakelike Dragon. She wished *anyone* was there, to help blunt the desperate feeling of being so entirely alone. At last she realized it was Phoebe she was wishing for. *Because,* she reasoned, *if Phoebe was here, it would either mean we've already rescued her, or, better still, that we never had to go.* And thinking of Phoebe, she felt sicker than ever. If she was honest with herself (and Sadie always tried to be honest) she did not want to go to Dragonland at all.

In all honesty, she was terrified. It was hard to breathe, as if her throat were constricting with fear. Or, she thought with a sudden rush of terror, it might have been the altitude. Looking down the impossible distance to the earth, she realized the air was only going to get thinner if they continued flying up. "I can't breathe!" she called out with what seemed to be her last lungful of air, but the Dragon seemed to understand. She turned her head and blew, and Sadie found herself surrounded by a bubble of smoke that trapped the air around her like a cocoon. Inside it, she felt strangely safer, despite the dismaying sight of the ever-receding Earth down below her.

And then, through the thin walls of that smoke cocoon, she saw an amazing sight: the sudden falling of night as they left the Earth's atmosphere. The sun falls on all the solar system as it falls on Earth, but it is only our air that bends the light and makes our sky that familiar bowl of blue. Now, as Sadie and the Dragon burst through the last of the atmosphere, the blue was suddenly replaced by black. Wordlessly, Sadie looked around. It was the most beautiful and melancholy sight she'd ever seen. The black expanse of night stretched all around them, with the sun of day blazing away in the middle of it. Then, to her left, she saw a blank spot in the field of stars, a place where no lights twinkled, and they were hurtling towards it, eel-like, into the middle of that blackness. Suddenly, impossibly, they broke into the blazing yellow sky of another world. Sadie gasped: for the first time she was seeing the rocky crags of the mountains of Dragonland.

"What—what just happened?" she asked.

The Dragon stopped blowing out smoke long enough to answer, and they lurched down towards the gray and foamy sea that stretched between them and the mountains.

"It is the Portal," she explained, "a hole through space that somehow links our world to yours. My People have been traveling through it since time immemorial."

Sadie looked down nervously at the waters below them. With trepidation, she stared at the dark mass of some *thing* that moved under the heaving seas, and she begged the Dragon to stop talking and start flying again.

They skimmed along thirty feet above the water as if carried on the waves. Sadie's brain scrambled to understand what she was seeing, and failed miserably. At the same time, she was far too practical to doubt that she was in fact on another planet. It was the simplest explanation, after all, for everything was slightly alien, slightly wrong. The orange sun hung large and menacing in the yellowish sky, and to her surprise Sadie saw another whitish spot, like a second sun, burning through the clouds, the way a bright comet shines feebly in the daylight.

"How are you doing, Sadie?" the Dragon asked roughly, sending them falling closer to the waters again. "I am dying for a rest; I think we will take it on that rock."

In Sadie's opinion, the place the Dragon indicated was hardly a rock: just a few jagged spikes that had been thrust out of the waves in some distant volcanic eruption. The Dragon landed on it, gave a great wheezing cough, and sagged a little as Sadie slipped off her back.

"I am out of condition," she muttered. "I have lived too long in human form. It is a limited shape, much prone to cramping, and now that I have the freedom to stretch and fly, I discover that I have grown old." She looked out over the swelling sea towards the distant mountains and sighed philosophically. "But there is some consolation in that: at least it will not be long before I will have my chance to lie down in the river and extinguish the fire that has been consuming me for so long."

"Your fire?" Sadie asked curiously. "You mean it hurts you?"

"Of course it hurts me, child!" the Dragon replied in Mrs.

Fitz Edna's sharpest voice. "It burns within me night and day. Even in my sleep I dream of fire." She shook her heavy head philosophically. "But that is what it means to be one of the People. When we are young, and the smoke that comes from our noses is white, we long for the fire. But that is what youth is—the desire for the responsibilities of age without understanding the pain. All through our youth we look with eagerness to see if our smoke is burning gray, so we can leave the River Time of youth for the Mountain Time of adulthood, but we do not understand what it means."

Sadie's mind boggled; for the first time she wished she'd paid more attention to Phoebe's Dragon stories. "What's that, the Mountain Time?" she asked.

"It is what it says it is. After we visit the sacred pools to lay our clutches of eggs and say good-bye to childhood, we journey to the stone houses up on the mountain peaks. There we would freeze were it not for our fires. But we have no fire, not yet, and to keep alive we must focus all our attention on awakening the fire within. A few do not make it, of course—they curl up there, and die. It is so cold, you see—so very cold—you have never felt a cold like it. It is our trial, to sit up there, crouching in a corner on the flagstone floor that feels like ice, and worrying that it is we who will not be able to awaken our flame."

"Why don't you just go back to the rivers, then?" asked Sadie practically.

"Because we have been locked in," the Dragon replied. "The door is made of the thickest wood, and there is no handle, no hinges, on the inside. There is only one way out, and that is to burn the door down. But we have no fire with which to burn the wood. Slowly, we start to freeze. The cold is crueler by the day. We curse it. We curse the cold with all the names we can think of, but of course the cold doesn't care. As we say, 'The coldness is nothing, and nothingness is the coldest of all.'"

"Oh," said Sadie, shivering as a gray wave pitched over the edge of the rock and splashed her feet.

The Dragon went on. "And then we think of the days we lay basking in the sun, and the way the light bounced from the River Yrcxg, and how happy we were among our family in the beautiful city of Xthltg, and how we never realized it before. The Mountain Time is good for that, as well, to make us think of the happiness in small things, to promise that we will savor each moment, if only we can escape from the crushing cold. And that is a thought that makes our fires burn a little warmer. And we think of our enemies who would destroy it all, and that makes the fire burn brightest of all. And then, just as we have given ourselves up for lost, we see that the smoke that pours from our noses is black, the most glorious of blacks, and then, little Sadie, *then* comes the moment that the fire leaps into its own, and from the pain deep inside we know we are saved, and we let lose a great cry, like this!" The

Dragon opened her mouth. Sadie jumped back as the orange flames flew forward thirty feet, and only just managed to keep herself from falling into the inhospitable sea. But in a way it was lucky that she lost her balance, for it allowed her to catch sight of the unwanted *something*—the black moving *something*—that was coming near them under the shifting surface of the water.

"We let out our cry," the Dragon repeated triumphantly, "we let it loose, and then, and then! The door bursts into flame, and burns from its hinges, and then Mountain Time is over, and we shall never be cold again! And then, Sadie, then, we know that at last we can fly—"

"Flying . . . that's a good idea," said Sadie distractedly, staring at the black shadow that was circling about them under the waters. It was enormously long and sleek, and the teeth in its open mouth were very long. Sadie caught sight of its evil eye, like the dead eye of a shark, and shook the Dragon by the shoulder. "Uh . . . Dra . . . Mrs. Fi . . . look . . ."

"Yes," agreed the Dragon, ignoring Sadie's pointing finger, "it is wonderful to fly, but the fire is also a constant pain. And now that my Princess is in trouble, the burning within me is almost unbearable."

"Mrs. Fitz Edna," Sadie cried, for lack of a better name to get the Dragon's attention. "What *is* that thing?" The monster was more than a shadow under the waves now—Sadie could see its white belly and the long flippers that could easily knock them into the waves if the sharp teeth did not finish them first. She had never been so frightened in her life: she knew at that moment that the worst stage fright is nothing compared to the physical fear of death as it approaches you with open jaws.

The Dragon raised her head, and her eyes fixed on the black mass moving towards them. "There is no rest for the weary," she said with a sigh. "It is a good human expression. Come, Sadie. Climb up on my back. It seems it is our lot to fly from danger to danger."

They took off from the rock in a roar of smoke and fire, but Sadie's quick knots were not tight enough, and she found herself slipping, not off the Dragon, but beneath her belly, and she dangled there, too close to the waves, just inches above that hungry *something* that lurched out of the waters. Then the Dragon put on another burst of speed, and the enormous mouth sank disappointed beneath the waves. Sadie closed her eyes and wished fervently that she was dreaming.

"What *was* that?" she burst out when she finally managed to climb back on top of the Dragon.

"We call it a Krnsrs," the Dragon who had once been Mrs. Fitz Edna replied, sending them dipping towards the waves. "You are not on Earth any longer, little Sadie, and here there are monsters. Yes, monsters; the Krnsrs is the least of them. I fear we will have to confront far worse before our journey has ended."

Sadie stared miserably down at the gray waters.

"I think I want to go home," she said.

"Nonsense," the Dragon chided gently, and once more they shot off towards land.

Phoebe had always talked about Dragonland as if it were the most beautiful place imaginable, with the silver moongrass and the little white starflowers, the crystal rocks, and the great spreading trees where white giraffes grazed, but even when they reached the land, that was not what Sadie saw. The beach below them seemed to be covered not by sand but by some squat and fleshy gray plants, looking and smelling something like decaying sea anemones. But the Dragon that had so recently been Mrs. Fitz Edna did not seem disgusted; she took a deep breath and gave a little sigh that sounded something like *"Home"* before shooting forward with renewed purpose.

But then, just before they reached the mountains, the Dragon let out a keening wail. The sound of it bounced off the mountains and rang in Sadie's ears like the sudden mourning of an entire race.

"What is it?" she cried. "What is it?"

The Dragon did not answer. Turning, and letting out a desperate shriek of smoke, she shot on towards the mountain, landing on a cliff with a heavy thud. Sadie stared. This was not Pheobe's lovely Dragonland, either. The flat desolate valley below them was the ugliest place Sadie had ever seen. There was no color at all. The mountains that ringed the valley were a dark and gravestone gray, each carved by time into menacing spires. In the shadowed valley below, all was still, except the faint movement of water. The Dragon beneath her crumpled to her knees.

"They have killed it," she said in a tone of doleful finality.

4

Xthltg

Sadie peered over the edge of the crag. A ray of feeble sunlight somehow managed to work its way between two of the
mountains, and Sadie saw that what she was looking at was
a lake, glinting like gunmetal in the gloom. As her eyes grew
accustomed to the thin and grainy light, she saw that the
shapes that broke through its surface had once been the tops
of buildings.

"What happened?" she asked in a horrified whisper.

"This was Xthltg," the Dragon answered mournfully. Sadie
had never seen anyone look so defeated. "It was the greatest
city of my People. And now . . ."

"But what *happened?*" Sadie asked again.

"I saw it when we came over the sea, that the River Yrcxg no longer ran to its home. From time out of mind, the river flowed from the top of the mountains, and it flowed down into the valley. It was our sacred river—its banks were lined with temples where the children would live before they reached the age of Graysmoke. 'Water protects where fire burns not'; that's what we always said. And now water has destroyed Xthltg. The Barbazion have used our sacred river to destroy us."

From far below, the wind whistled in the ruins.

"I still don't understand," said Sadie, staring down at the desolation.

"The Barbazion dammed up our river," the Dragon cried out bitterly. "The Barbazion dammed it up, and they have killed Xthltg with the river meant to protect it."

It was horrible to see a fellow creature in such distress, even one so strange and alien as the Dragon. Sadie reached out a tentative hand, and the Dragon turned to her with mournful eyes—Mrs. Fitz Edna's eyes. Suddenly Sadie knew it didn't matter that the Dragon beside her didn't look like an old lady with nicotine-stained fingers and an untidy cardigan. She was the same Mrs. Fitz Edna as always, and Sadie still loved her.

But Mrs. Fitz Edna seemed changed, beaten down by the sight before them, and it made Sadie feel desperate. This was the same Mrs. Fitz Edna, after all, who ordered Sadie to fight for justice wherever she could; the same Mrs. Fitz Edna who taught her not to cry over spilled milk, to turn lemons into lemonade, and to always remember that where there's a will there's a way. She wouldn't ever accept a defeat like this—Sadie just needed to remind her.

"It couldn't have filled up very quickly," she said, trying to look on the bright side of things. "The others must have had time to escape."

"You don't understand," Mrs. Fitz Edna said, weeping, and in this she was right. "Even if every one of my People had died pierced by a Barbazion arrow, it would not have mattered: the river would still have flowed. This, this . . . it's more than I can bear." She pulled back her head then and let out a howl of outrage and misery and loneliness and impotence and fury, and Sadie saw the streaks of fire that shot from her throat into the dimness. Then Mrs. Fitz Edna hung down her head and let out a mournful breath of smoke. "It is true, then, what they say. There is no evil of which the Barbazion are not capable."

"Mrs. Fitz Edna . . ." Sadie began tentatively, like someone compelled to ask a question best left unanswered, ". . . who are the Barbazion?"

"Oh, Sadie, poor Sadie—I forgot you did not know. For so long I have thought of you as one of my own hatchlings that there are times I forget that you are still an ignorant human. And young, so young. . . ."

"What are they? Are they Dragons, too?"

"Dragons!" Mrs. Fitz Edna burst out. "*I* am not a Dragon,

either, as you think of it—I am one of the People. But the Barbazion are not *people*—they are hideous monsters. The sun itself turns its face when they show their grotesque forms. They lurk in the dark, lurking, lurking, preying on the weak and exploiting every advantage." She held out her elegant claws, imitating how the Barbazion might snatch a little Dragon about the neck, and Sadie shuddered. "They delight in cruelty, Sadie. They like nothing better than causing pain, especially to the People. No, Sadie. Nothing on Earth prepared you for monsters such as they."

Sadie shivered. The fear that had not entirely left her since the morning intensified painfully inside her. But Sadie did not like to be frightened, and she had long figured out how to turn to fear into anger. Now her anger burst out as indignation.

"How dare they!" she raged, pointing down to the slowly swirling waters of the lake.

Mrs. Fitz Edna lifted her grave face towards Sadie's, and the faint fire in her eyes matched the one that had been lit by indignation in Sadie's heart.

"They dared because they saw our weakness. The Prophecy is very clear: 'Whoever controls the Princess commands victory.' Now *they* have captured the Princess, and now they have nothing to fear from us. Oh, we have taken a wrong turn somewhere—we now walk on an evil path."

"What Princess? What Prophecy?"

"Forgive me—I keep forgetting. It was a prophecy made ten thousand years ago: *A golden egg laid in a litter of leaves, born in darkness on the first bright day of spring, born in darkness to everlasting light.* That is the Prophecy. It took our scholars millennia to understand it. But as with all truths, it is crystal clear when you see it at last: a golden egg will hatch on the first day of spring and lead us to a time when we do not have to fear the dark—that is, when we do not have to fear the Barbazion. But many hatchlings have clawed their ways out of golden eggs, and many on the first day of spring, but still we could not drive the Barbazion from our lands. But then, on the first day of spring not many years ago, we were astounded to see the sun blotted from the sky."

"An eclipse?" asked Sadie.

Mrs. Fitz Edna nodded. "The sun was not gone from the sky long," she said, "but in that time, a golden egg began to roll with the struggle of hatching, and while the sky was still dark, our Princess crept forth from her egg. She was strange and soft, with no tail and no scales, but to us she was glorious, for at last the Prophecy was fulfilled."

Mrs. Fitz Edna paused. "There was great rejoicing among my People, then, Sadie—for it seemed possible we would finally be able to throw off the yoke of fear that the Barbazion have long laid around our necks. But we were not the only ones to know about the Prophecy." She stopped then, and looked out over the destruction of the city.

"The Barbazion came to us, in the days after the sun was blotted from the sky. They spoke to us of their own prophecy, and demanded we turn the child over to them. For they, too, knew that whoever led their armies with the Princess in their care would be invincible. There was an uneasy peace between the People and the Barbazion for a thousand years, Sadie, for both sides knew there would be much killing and no victory, not until the Prophecy was fulfilled. But once the Princess was born (May Fire and Water Protect Her), the Barbazion began to move against us, for they knew that with the Prophecy fulfilled, there could at last be a final victory for our side—or for theirs. But we knew there would be no victory for us if she were captured by the Barbazion, and we knew that though the fire would someday burn within her, she was for the moment left without even the most rudimentary defenses of our People. In the end, there was only one thing to do. We must take her and hide her among those who looked enough like her, those on the other side of the Portal. And so we sent her to live with a family where she would be safe. *Now* do you understand, Sadie?"

It was just like the moment when she'd seen the smoke pouring out of Mrs. Fitz Edna in Phoebe's bedroom. Sadie understood, but she did not want to understand.

"Phoebe," she started. "You can't be talking about Phoebe! Phoebe's not a Dra . . ."

Mrs. Fitz Edna interrupted patiently. "As I told you, I am

not a Dragon either, though Phoebe, with her limited vocabulary, called me so. I am one of the People, and so is our Phoebe, though she looks more like one of you little humans. That is the truth, Sadie. Phoebe's name may be Phoebe on Earth, but she is truly called Xthpqltthpqlwxn. She is one of the People, and not truly your sister."

Sadie had no answer to that. She thought about Phoebe and all the times they had played together, and the times they had fought; the cozy family time, the vacation time, the holiday time, the quiet times when they had sat side by side in the back of the car, comfortable together though each alone with her thoughts. She thought of the last time she had seen Phoebe, standing in her door and demanding the family blessing of "be safe," and she knew that Mrs. Fitz Edna was decidedly wrong.

"No," she said firmly. "Phoebe *is* my sister."

"Child, child, haven't you understood anything I've told you? Xthpqltthpqlwxn is not human. In fact, she is one of my own great-great-grandchildren. . . ."

"I don't care," Sadie declared. "She *is* my sister, regardless, and I'm going to find her and bring her home."

Mrs. Fitz Edna's eyes filled with tears. "We chose well," she said to the heavens. "I always told the Council that *your* family would be best. Loyalty, courage, determination, I said. That's what Sadie has and, as I said, my dear, we will all count on those qualities in the coming days."

"Well, what are we waiting for?" Sadie demanded. "Let's go get Phoebe!"

But instead of moving, Mrs. Fitz Edna stared at Sadie with sorrowful eyes. "Don't you understand? Unless I am very much mistaken, our Phoebe is being held captive by the Barbazion."

5

The Barbazion

They were flying again. Sadie pressed her face into Mrs. Fitz Edna's back and tried not to look at the landscape that streaked below them. Phoebe, captured by the Barbazion: she tried not to think of that. She was no longer on the same planet as her parents—she tried not to think at all. But try as she might, all she could hear in the whistling of the wind was a cackle of evil laughter: *Your sister is in our hands. You, just you, you and only you in your lonely alone loneliness,* you, *Sadie Ann Guthrie, you are the only one who can save her.*

Mrs. Fitz Edna was not much comfort, either. She stopped again and again to rest, and Sadie saw that each time she climbed back onto the Dragon's back, Mrs. Fitz Edna groaned a little, and seemed to sag. It pained her to see the Dragon so tired, and at one stop she turned to Mrs. Fitz Edna with anxious concern.

"Can't I walk?" she asked. "Is it much farther?"

"I cannot answer that question without knowing the future," Mrs. Fitz Edna replied. "We have a saying: 'The length of a journey depends always on what you find along the way.' If we reach the pools of Frthgl and they are abandoned, for example, we will be forced to go on. In such a way, the journey may be much longer than we expected. On the other hand, if we are ambushed by the Barbazion, our journey may be very short indeed."

"What *are* those pools?" Sadie asked, to get Mrs. Fitz Edna off the subject of being ambushed.

"They are on the slopes of the Flat Mountain, the mountain we call the Mother of Fire, though it has slept for many years. My People have always gone there to lay our eggs in that sacred place. It is far too remote for the Barbazion to reach—at least, they have never traveled so far south before. It is my hope that we will be safe there."

Her voice grew more gentle then. "I will be glad to show you something lovely of my world, Sadie," she said. "There is no place more soothing and peaceful than those pools—their smell is like the sweetest baby's breath. We will rest up there for the struggles ahead." She sighed. "I find I need the rest— I am far older than I ever remember feeling before."

"You're not old!" Sadie corrected, just as she had done each time the human Mrs. Fitz Edna had complained about climbing the grand library steps.

"There is no point in deceiving ourselves," the Dragon reproached her gently. "I *am* old. I am very old. I was chosen for my mission because of my age, you see, and my strength has been greatly spent by the transformation that made me appear human."

"Can Dragons do magic, then?" Sadie asked hopefully.

Mrs. Fitz Edna blew out a little wisp of impatient smoke. "As I have told you, Sadie, we are not Dragons—we are the People. And the People have no magic as you wish we had. We can understand the language of all creatures, of course, but that is no more magic than the fact that fish can breathe underwater: it is the way of things. Our one magic, if you want to call it so, is that—through enormous effort—we can take other forms once our fires have burned enough of our true natures away. Once many of us could do this, but since the war with the Barbazion began in earnest, I am the only one left who is old enough to take on that task. That is why I was sent to guard over the Princess (May Fire and Water Protect Her)."

"I'm glad," Sadie said, pressing the Dragon's arm. "I'm glad it was you."

"As was I, little Sadie," said Mrs. Fitz Edna tenderly. "I was glad until this morning when I found the Princess gone, but since then I am only weary. The trip through the Portal was my second, and at my age I should not have attempted it twice. It is a hard journey—even those who carried the basket came four times and no more, or risked never flying again. It takes too much out of us, and now I find what little I had is almost gone."

"I wish I could help you," Sadie whispered.

"You will," answered Mrs. Fitz Edna grimly. "There was good reason the Princess was placed with you. May Fire and Water Protect Her, now that she is out of your care. Come now; we have long to go, and we have rested too long."

They came across the other Dragons just as the sun was setting behind the hill. There were ten or twelve of them, at least—in the dim light and the great quantity of smoke, Sadie wasn't quite sure if she could tell where one tail ended and another body began. But there were a lot of them, and they all seemed very agitated. To Sadie's frustration, she found she could not understand a single thing they said, not even Mrs. Fitz Edna. It wasn't just that they were speaking a different language, either: it was as if the sounds they made couldn't fit inside her human ears. Nevertheless, from the slow shaking of the heavy heads, she guessed they were talking of the destruction of Xthltg and of comrades who would never fly overhead again; from the curious looks they aimed towards Sadie, she guessed Mrs. Fitz Edna was explaining who she was. The one word she could make sense of was the repeated "Barbazion"—

Brbz'n, Brbz'n, Brbz'n. Each time she heard it, it felt like a punch to the stomach.

The sun was setting now. Sadie felt the hairs on her neck prickling, especially when her back was to the forest. Mrs. Fitz Edna had told her the Barbazion came out only at night, and it was now coming close to evening. She touched the Dragon's shoulder to get her attention, to remind her they should hurry to the sweet-smelling pools of Frthgl where they would be safe, but Mrs. Fitz Edna ignored her the way grown-ups always ignore children when they are very worried. One of the other Dragons was speaking seriously. When it finished, the assembly paused for a moment and spit out fire in unison, as if making an oath. Then Mrs. Fitz Edna turned back to Sadie.

"We go," she said curtly. Without saying good-bye to the other Dragons, she waited for Sadie to climb on her back again, and together they streaked away into the darkness, lower now, as if Mrs. Fitz Edna did not have the energy to fly higher in the sky.

Sadie looked down at the landscape that flew backwards beneath them. The light was dim, but she could still make out the rolling hills, and then a great patch of moving white. She stared. It moved like a herd—it was a herd. Enormous creatures, as much bigger than an elephant as an elephant is bigger than a lion, with great white towering necks—Phoebe's white giraffes. They were galloping, galloping across the rolling plains, twitching their ears with the pleasure of their running, and even from the air, Sadie could hear the thunder of their feet. It was a glorious sight, one Sadie wished she could watch forever, but then they were gone.

The hills gave way to forests. The trees were a sea of black now in the gathering dusk, but Sadie could see more animals that crept from their shade to graze in the crepuscular light. There were animals with great spreading horns, horns so outrageously outsized that they looked as if the antlers of a moose had been placed on the head of a cat. Then there was another creature, furry like a bear, but many-legged, like a centipede, that glided over the grass; and then there were lurking shapes, crocodilian, that suddenly lunged at the others, scattering the peace and sending the birds flying into the sky.

Sadie shuddered. To her dismay, they were landing again. Mrs. Fitz Edna set down on a craggy rock, half-covered with small trees. Sadie looked around them anxiously. It was very dark now, except for the moon and the red light that seemed to come from Mrs. Fitz Edna's eyes.

"Those crocodile things . . ." she started. "Those weren't the Barbazion, were they?"

Mrs. Fitz Edna shook her head. She coughed twice, and seemed to be struggling to catch her breath. Sadie climbed guiltily down from her back.

"Sentiment," the Dragon muttered. "I should have let one of the others carry you towards Frthgl, but sentiment blinded me to my weakness." She coughed again, and the smoke that came from her mouth seemed to Sadie to be tinged with red.

"What did the other Dragons tell you?" Sadie asked, still nervously looking over her shoulder into the darkness.

Mrs. Fitz Edna gave her a quizzical look. "Of course," she sighed at last. "You couldn't understand them. I must be getting old to forget such a complication. . . ." She shook her head, but then, as if steeling her resolve, she smiled grimly. "My People have a saying: 'A one-legged creature would be grateful to have three legs to walk upon.' That is us, for we have something to be grateful for: at least you and I can speak to each other. As to what the others said, it grieves me too much to repeat it. But I did hear one piece of glad news: my great-grandson Xpql was last seen near Frthgl. I thought he would have gone to the mountains by now, but apparently he is still a Graysmoke, and we should be able to find him there."

"Are the others going to meet us there, too?"

"No—the others are going closer to the Glass Castle of the Barbazion," Mrs. Fitz Edna explained, wincing a little as she moved her sore hips.

"The Glass Castle?" Sadie asked, and then she remembered the story Phoebe had told that last morning, yesterday morning, that yesterday morning a hundred years ago—how the basket-carrying Dragons had gone too close to a castle of black glass, with a roving red light on its top.

"Yes," Mrs. Fitz Edna confirmed. "That is the castle of the

Princess's story, May Fire and Water Protect Her. The basket-carriers flew too close, I fear. Since the moment I heard Xthpqltthpqlwxn's story, I feared that the Barbazion saw them. Until that moment, they might have believed, as we wished them to believe, that she was held somewhere in Xthltg. That must be why they moved against us so recently: they never would have dared destroy the city if they thought the Princess might be inside it. They will not wish her harm, for they cannot hope to defeat us without her, as without her we cannot hope to defeat them. But now that they have her, I fear my People may be utterly destroyed. There has never been a time the Barbazion have suffered one of the People to live once in their power, unless it has been to use them as the basest of slaves."

"Oh, *Phoebe*," Sadie whispered. In her head she said a little prayer: *Be safe, be safe, be safe.* But in her heart, Sadie did not really believe in prayers, or in miracles either. In the end, if Phoebe was to be saved, it was her friends and family who would have to do it. And though Sadie was more frightened than she could have believed a person could be, there was no helping it. She had promised her parents she was going to protect Phoebe, and she was going to do it.

"We should go there, too," she said, with a deep breath. "We should go to the Glass Castle."

But Mrs. Fitz Edna shook her head. "I do not doubt your bravery," she said. "But it is not yet time—there is no point in risking you so early in the game. But when we call upon you, I am certain you will be able to do all that is required."

It was then they both heard it: a furtive crackling in the underbrush, as if something were creeping ever closer towards them up the side of the rock. Sadie turned to Mrs. Fitz Edna in fear.

"On my back, quickly!" the Dragon commanded, aiming a stream of fire into the brush. There was a howl and a scampering below them, but Mrs. Fitz Edna and Sadie were circling high above the forest, speeding on towards Frthgl. But though Mrs. Fitz Edna had moved vigorously to carry them away from the danger, Sadie could tell how much it had taken out of her. She was not surprised when they had to stop to rest shortly after.

Just before the sun set, Sadie saw that the horizon had gathered up into a hump in the distance. At last it took the shape of a mountain standing alone on the plain, its flat top making it look as if it had once thrown off its peak in a fit of volcanic fury. Mrs. Fitz Edna saw it, too, and with an extra burst of smoke and flame sent them faster towards it.

"Is that where we're going?" Sadie called, and Mrs. Fitz Edna nodded. The Dragon was panting now, her chest heaving between Sadie's knees, and now and then they slipped closer to the ground as her breath failed her. "Do you need to stop again?" Sadie called, but the Dragon shook her head. They flew on and on, but the mountain did not seem to get any closer, no matter how much Mrs. Fitz Edna panted.

The moon was up over the horizon when Sadie saw the lights. They were swarming below, like a colony of luminescent ants.

"Barbazion," Mrs. Fitz Edna hissed, and they lurched downwards for a moment.

"Shouldn't we go around?" Sadie whispered.

"I wish I had the strength," Mrs. Fitz Edna replied. They fell lower still with every word, and Sadie urged her not to speak anymore, especially because Mrs. Fitz Edna did not seem to have the breath to bring them upwards again. From their lower altitude, Sadie saw the lights came from the fire of torches, and she pressed her face into the scales of Mrs. Fitz Edna's neck, scarcely daring to breathe. From down below she could hear the shouts and cries of the Barbazion, and her eyes filled with tears.

I'm so scared, she thought. *Please, I want to go home.* But no booming voice answered her, no magic power transported her back to Earth. Then, despite her aching loneliness, despite the icy fear that seized her, another part of Sadie rose to the challenge—the part of her that claimed her body and squared her shoulders boldly when it was time for her to grab the rope at the quarry. *The one-legged creature would be glad to have three legs to walk upon,* she thought. *At least I have Mrs. Fitz Edna.* She leaned forward and kissed the rough scales of the neck, just below the head.

Mrs. Fitz Edna seemed to take strength from it. The bright lights below them were shrinking as the Dragon gave a last push towards the rising moon, and looking down, Sadie saw that they were almost to the edge of the dark blankness between the Barbazion and the mountain. "Come on, Mrs. Fitz Edna!" she whispered encouragingly. "We're almost there!" Mrs. Fitz Edna gave another tremendous burst, and they shot forward, towards the safety of the dark, the wind whistling in Sadie's ears like a wild melody. But then, in the middle of the song of the wind, she heard another sound: the twang of a bowstring, and the singing flight of an arrow. And just as she heard it, she felt it in her leg: first the pain of the impact, and then the burning of the shaft, and then, worst of all, the terrible feeling of falling as she and Mrs. Fitz Edna plummeted to the ground.

Painfully, Sadie woke up. Her head ached. Everything ached. She opened her eyes into the grainy grayness of moonlight, and saw the still shape of Mrs. Fitz Edna beside her. Wearily, painfully, she tried to get to her feet, but fell down with a yelp of pain. The arrow that had passed through her calf had pinned her to the Dragon.

"Mrs. Fitz Edna?" she whispered urgently.

The Dragon let off a stream of smoke, and coughed twice. She did not seem to have the strength to speak.

"Mrs. Fitz Edna!" Sadie cried. "Don't be hurt! Mrs. Fitz Edna! Mrs. Fitz Edna!"

The Dragon was breathing quickly now, but so shallowly her side barely moved under Sadie's hand. The light from her eyes was fading, and when she spoke, it was so quiet Sadie could barely hear it.

"You must find my grandson," the Dragon whispered in painful little gasps. "Find Xpql on the mountain. He will help you reach the Princess. . . ."

"No, no!" Sadie cried. "No, Mrs. Fitz Edna, *you* will help me! Don't talk like that! Don't!"

"Sadie," breathed the Dragon. Her eyes were closed, and Sadie felt in her bones how very hard it would be for Mrs. Fitz Edna to open them again. "You must go now, child. The Barbazion will be coming, and they *must* not catch you. The Princess needs you. . . ." She was breathing heavily now, painfully, and her breath was hot on Sadie's face. "Go. *Now.* Pull out the arrow, child. Pull it out and run. Run towards the moon and you will find the mountain, but don't let them catch you! Once you are at the mountain, you will find my grandson by the sweet smell of the pools. Run, Sadie! The Barbazion will be coming soon. *Run!* Everything depends on you."

"But *I* depend on *you*," Sadie wept, not only for the Dragon she needed to save her sister, but also for Mrs. Fitz Edna, who had been like a third parent to her, the parent who had always known her best.

"I have always liked your human sayings," said Mrs. Fitz Edna, gritting her teeth against the pain. "One that strikes me as true is 'You must cut your pants from the cloth you are given.' Go, now. Let me die knowing that my mission does not die with me."

"No," choked Sadie. "Not die, not *die*, Mrs. Fitz Edna, tell me you're not going to *die*."

"The Barbazion never suffer the People to live once in their hands," Mrs. Fitz Edna reminded her. "Run now, Sadie. I have no breath for arguments. Do this for me, if you love me."

Miserably, Sadie looked down at the arrow that protruded from her leg, and saw that though her own wound was superficial, the arrow had pierced Mrs. Fitz Edna in the breast.

"It will hurt you if I pull it out," she wept.

"It will hurt me more if the Barbazion catch you," the Dragon panted. Sadie laid her hand on the long shaft of the arrow, pulled her hand away, touched the wood again, and finally, with the same half-bravery, half-foolhardiness with which she had climbed onto Mrs. Fitz Edna's back in Phoebe's bedroom, she grabbed the arrow and yanked it out. Blood poured from Mrs. Fitz Edna's wound and sizzled onto the ground, and Sadie understood that the painful burning in her own wound was caused not only by the arrow but by the Dragon blood that had been mingling with her own.

She crouched down beside Mrs. Fitz Edna and kissed the heavy head. The pain in her leg felt like nothing next to her grief. "I'm so sorry," she stammered.

"Go," the Dragon answered.

"I don't know what to say. I can't believe I'm saying good-bye."

"Go!" repeated the Dragon. The smoke that came from her nostrils was thin and wispy now, like the smoke from a dying fire, and Sadie saw that the blood from the wound was leaking out in slow trickles, as if the great heart could barely pump any longer.

"There's so much I want to tell you—"

"Go!" whispered the Dragon, for the last time.

Sadie stood before her, the tears rolling down her face. In the distance, she heard the faint sound of movement heading towards them, and she knew she should run. But her grief was too heavy; it weighed her to the ground.

"I love you," she said at last. "And, and . . ." But there were no words to express what she wanted to say. They had never said good-bye before. They had said, "See you on Tuesday." They had said, "See you in the morning." They had said, "See you when we get back." She could not say good-bye, not if it was forever.

"Run," whispered the Dragon, so quietly that it might have been a single blade of grass blowing in the breeze. And Sadie, caught between her fear of the Barbazion and the misery that bound her to the dying Dragon, felt there was only one thing left to say.

"Be safe," she whispered. Then, miserably, agonizedly, wretchedly, she ran. She was not quite far enough away not to hear the shout of triumph that went up when the Barbazion reached Mrs. Fitz Edna's body.

6

The Bird

The suns were just breaking over the edge of the mountain when Sadie woke up from an uneasy sleep. The morning light made the mountain look more black and ominous than ever, but the place where she found herself was no more inviting. Sadie stood painfully and looked around her: in the dark, it appeared, she had stumbled into some sort of alien swamp. Little green pools glinted here and there in the early-morning light, and occasionally, subterranean gas burbled up and broke on the surface with a burst of fetid stench. Sadie picked her way through the wet places, ducking under the swamp plants, gray-green and sickly-looking. Some were covered with big, fleshy flowers that looked like hungry mouths, and when

Sadie screwed up her courage to look inside, she saw a small rodentlike creature there, twitching in its last unhappy throes. Once or twice she pricked herself on some long and spiky thorns, and they left red scratches that continued to burn long after.

Sadie soldiered on. Although Mrs. Fitz Edna had said that the Barbazion came out only at night, she felt horribly exposed in that barren landscape, especially as the suns grew higher in the sky. There were no trees in the stunted wasteland that surrounded her, no cover at all, except for the tall gray ferns that grew in clumps between the gray water of the pools. Sadie peered up into the yellowish sky. The larger of the two suns seemed to peer down on her like a watchful angry eye, and at every moment she expected a great finger to come out of the sky and point her out to her enemies, calling, *There she is! There's the human! Get her now, while she's defenseless.*

"Ha!" she said to herself. "When *won't* I be defenseless?" She looked down at her soft arms and legs, the blunt nails on her hands, and she ran her tongue over her flat teeth while tenderly feeling the wound on her calf. She thought of the Dragons, with their claws and fangs and fire, and of the fear they felt of the Barbazion. Suddenly, she couldn't stand it. The terrible hunted feeling made her whole body tense up with fear. Instinctively, she hurried towards the cover of the ferns.

She huddled in their shade, and the misery of her situation fell over her all at once.

"I'm going to die here, you know," she announced to anyone who was there to listen. "I'm going to die here, and Phoebe's going to die here, too, and no one will ever know what happened to us."

Something was stirring above her head. Looking up, Sadie saw a little creature, much like a sparrow, cocking its head at her and chirruping sympathetically. To Sadie's lonely ears, it sound like nothing more than *poor girl, poor girl, poor girl*.

Sadie smiled through her tears. There are birds on Earth whose calls seem to mimic words in English, like the *whip poor will* of the whip-poor-will, or the *teacher, teacher, teacher* of the ovenbird, or the *Peter, Peter* of the titmouse. But this bird was looking down at Sadie and saying *poor girl, poor girl, poor girl* in mournful tones, and even through her misery, Sadie laughed. With the sudden appearance of a companion, her plight did not seem quite so desperate—even her injured calf did not hurt so very much. But just as she was going to mention this to her new companion, the bird's chattering changed. Now it sounded like nothing so much as *Get up! Get up! Get up!* With horror, Sadie sprang to her feet. A fiddlehead fern was slowly uncoiling and reaching out towards her.

With a shriek, Sadie leapt from her seat into the stagnant pool beside her, while the fern snatched blindly at the place she had just been. But she could not rest. Something unwholesome was touching her foot under the water, and she leapt out of the pool and into a thornbush. Rubbing her arms to erase the fiery memory of the thorn, she bounced pinball-like against one of the carnivorous flowers, then bounded away when its heavy, cadaverous fingers touched her bare arm. She stumbled into another clump of ferns, which immediately began to uncoil and move towards her, and from there jumped just shy of a boiling pool. Finally she landed on a little hummock of dry grass, where she could stare back at the hall of horrors she had just passed through. A flutter of wings then, and the little bird landed on her shoulder, whistling its sympathetic call: *poor girl, poor girl, poor girl.*

"You said it, bird," said Sadie wryly. Then she laughed, though it was decidedly not funny. "Oh, Phoebe," she said to the heavens, "I've got to say you totally misrepresented Dragonland. When I find you . . ."

But that moment seemed impossibly far off. Ruefully Sadie looked up at the orange sun, which was now far past its zenith, and gauged the infinite distance to the mountain. She sighed.

"Well, we better go, bird," she said. "We better get to the mountain before the Barbazion come out."

Carefully, she picked her way through the swamp. The bird alternately rode on her shoulder and fluttered on ahead, as the mountain cast its dark shadow over them.

"Well, bird," Sadie went on. "Well, bird, I gotta say, I never thought I'd be in this situation. My friend Picker, now, *he's* the one who should be here. He's read the sort of books that would prepare him for this. I tell you, I'll never make fun of him for reading fantasy novels again—if I ever get back to see him, that is."

The bird whistled again, and Sadie, who had discovered that the sound of a human voice made her feel braver (even if it was only her own) went on.

"Is that really a black butterfly over there? This place is just too much. Look at him, bird, he's the size of a bat! But just a second, what did Phoebe say about black butterflies? She said they were good luck—'ashes of fire,' that's what she said." But thinking of Phoebe was a mistake; it only made her think painfully of Mrs. Fitz Edna and the lurking Barbazion, and her overtaxed heart was wrenched by fury, grief, and fear.

"I won't let them win," she said fiercely to the bird. "I *won't* let the Barbazion hurt my sister. I'm going to find them and rescue her, and then I will *avenge* Mrs. Fitz Edna. I was brought here for a reason, and this was it. I swear it, bird. I will help the Dragons wipe the Barbazion from the planet."

The bird whistled again, and, full of new purpose, Sadie took ever bigger strides towards the mountain.

They reached the bottom of its slopes before dark, and slowly began their perilous climb.

"It's a good thing I like you, bird," said Sadie as she panted along behind her feathered companion. "You're showing off, flying like that when I have to practically crawl up on the side."

The bird seemed to understand, and stayed by her side until they reached a flatter place. A river flowed there, cool, blue, and delightful, falling over the mossy rocks with a merry chuckle, and Sadie fell to her knees and plunged her face into it. The sweet water filled her belly like food and drink together, and at last she lay down beside it, eyes closed, her sore feet bathing in the running river. The water ran over her hurt calf like a gentle caress, and in the coolness of the water, most of the pain left her leg.

"Look at that," she wondered to the bird. "The wound's all closed—it's like magic." A sudden idea struck her. "Do you think it was the Dragon blood, bird? Could Mrs. Fitz Edna's blood be helping me? I certainly could use all the help I can get. We have to find the pools of something or other— we're supposed to know them by their sweet smell. But I think I have to rest a little longer. . . ."

But she could not rest long, for suddenly the bird, seeing something in the woods, gave a sudden frightened call that sounded like nothing so much as *Barbazion!* Sadie jumped up, looked around, and saw nothing but a shadow of a small cat-sized animal, lynxlike and low to the ground, crouching towards them. She reached down, picked up a rock, and threw it at the lynx. It sauntered away, unhurt, with a catlike shrug of its shoulders that said, *You aren't making me go; I am going of my own accord.*

"Stay away from my bird!" Sadie called after it angrily, while the bird chattered noisily from the safety of Sadie's shoulder.

"Don't scare me like that," she scolded the bird. "My heart's been beating so fast already, I think I've used up several years' worth of beats today. But I suppose it's not your fault—a cat like that must seem like a monster to you." She leaned back against the tree, smelling the clean smell of water, and closed her eyes. The bird sat on the ground beside her, pecking at a small woody cone filled with seeds. Then it pecked against Sadie's hand.

"What is it?"

Food-to-eat, food-to-eat, said the bird, and Sadie reached down and looked at the plump seeds. Gingerly, she tasted one with her tongue: it tasted of sweet almond, and she put it into her mouth and chewed first one and then another, and then a handful. She felt among the fallen leaves for more cones, and there, in the dark, she and the bird ate.

Slowly, the moon rose. It sent its silver light between the trunks, and it fell on the little bird as it ate its seeds. Sadie was about to reach out her hand to stroke its soft feathers when there was a sudden commotion. When she could make sense of the scene again, the bird was gone, except for a few feathers between the paws of the lynx.

"Barbazion," it said to her accusingly.

For a moment Sadie was so angry and full of grief she could not find her voice. Hatred for the lynx seemed to choke the air from her lungs.

"Barbazion?" she cried at last. "I'm not the monster, you

are, you, you . . ." but words failed her, and her throat tightened with grief.

"You could not keep me from my dinner, Barbazion," the animal growled at her, and then it sped into the darkness.

"I hate you!" she screamed, throwing cone after cone at the retreating cat, piling onto its arched back all her fury at the Barbazion as well as her grief for the bird. "I hate you! I hate this place! And it *stinks!*" It was true: the stench of sulfur was everywhere.

Sadie sat down heavily against the tree. If she had been the sort to cry, she would have cried then. Instead, she stared in stony silence out into the dark until at last, she slept.

7

Xpql

Sadie opened her eyes. A gray mist was seeping between the trees, and it carried on it the smell of sulfur. Sadie sat still for a moment, hunched against the tree. A few brown feathers were still scattered on the ground, and she picked one up and smoothed it out. *Oh, Phoebe!* she thought. *How can I protect you in the Glass Castle when I couldn't even protect this poor little bird next to me?*

But Sadie was not one to brood, and she was one to work. The fire of justice and revenge was upon her with full force. Her father always said he pitied the poor sap who offended Sadie's indefatigable sense of justice, and the Barbazion had done that now, far more than the causes she had crusaded for in the past. She had a death to avenge now—two, if you counted the bird, which Sadie most definitely did. She marched up the mountain full of purpose. Twice she thought she saw the slinking shape of the cat lurking in the trees, and she threw rocks at it and cursed its name. She felt such a hot anger burning in her that she almost felt like a Dragon herself.

But if she had become a Dragon, it appeared she was the only one on that mountain. The morning passed by, the mist burned off, and still she was alone in the sulfurous stench. She wandered ever upwards, with no one to complain to about the smell, or her wound, or the whole terrible situation. When the hot sun was directly overhead, she sat at the edge of the river and soaked her sore leg in the cool waters. The place where the arrow had pierced her only a day before was already healed over, the scar beginning to fade to silver, and she wondered again if the Dragon's blood that had dripped into her had helped cure the wound. And then, thinking of Dragon's blood and its purported properties, she remembered the story Phoebe was always demanding from Mrs. Fitz Edna: the story of Sigurd, who drank the Dragon Fafner's blood and gained the power to understand the animals.

Maybe it was true. She *had* understood the cat, after all. The cat had not said "Meow" or "Yeow" or whatever it was wildcats said on whatever planet she now found herself on: it had clearly said "Barbazion"—said it as clearly as if it had been speaking English. Of course, Mrs. Fitz Edna had insisted she and her

People were not Dragons, but then again, she had said that they had often traveled through the Portal in the past. Who knew what humans had seen them? Who knew how many myths had been sown by the appearance of Mrs. Fitz Edna and her kind among the people of superstitious Earth? Many disparate people had dragons, after all, and many had unicorns; perhaps all those stories had started with visitors from Dragonland.

And (she thought) there was a way to test her theory. She cocked her head towards the trees and listened for the birds as they went about their small business. There! She *could* understand them! They were arguing about the nest: it was all as clear as day.

You call that *a nest?*

If it was good enough for my mother, it should be good enough for you. This is how my father always made them.

It figures—your father was a lunkhead.

Sadie grinned. One problem, at least, was solved—if she ever found another Dragon on that mountain, she would be able to talk with it. "If the one-legged creature would be glad to have three legs to walk on, then he would be jealous of me," she said to the trees, to the sky, and most of all to herself. Then she began to trudge up the mountain once more.

Despite her renewed optimism, it was not a pleasant walk. The smell of sulfur was stronger that ever, and once she saw a small geyser spewing foul-smelling water into the air.

"What a *stink!*" she complained to the breeze. "*This* certainly isn't as sweet as a baby's breath!" And she held her nose, even if there was no one there to see the gesture.

The smell grew stronger as she headed for the mountain's flat top, avoiding the places where hot trickles of yellowish water came dribbling down the rocks, and recoiling when she saw the scalded corpse of a strange starfishlike creature beside another hot spring. Then, just as she was about to give up hope that she would ever find her destination, she came around a boulder and saw it: three steaming pools, bubbles breaking gently on the surface. Their colors were reflected on the white steam that floated above them: green, yellow, red, and blue—it was very beautiful. At that moment, a malodorous bubble burst, releasing its sulfur stink, and then Sadie understood. It *did* smell as sweet as a baby's breath there, she realized—as long as the baby to which you referred was a Dragon.

"Hello?" she called. There was a dark cave behind the steaming pools; a little white smoke drifted from it.

"Hello?" she called again.

A fearsome head poked out of the cave: a head with bulging gold eyes and two long barbels that hung from its ponderous chin. Two enormous fangs protruded from the mouth, but Sadie nearly rushed to the creature in relief. It was a Dragon, and the most beautiful sight Sadie's lonely eyes had ever seen.

"Thank goodness!" she cried. "Are you Xpql?"

The Dragon assented with a blink of his heavy eyelids. Then he turned around and withdrew his head. Slightly bewildered, Sadie followed him into the cave.

It was very spacious inside. As her eyes grew used to the dim light, Sadie saw that someone had arranged a spiral of rocks on the sandy floor, starting with a pebble in the very middle and working up to sizable rocks along the spiral's outer edge. Some of the stones looked very heavy, and Sadie watched with amazement as Xpql picked up one in his enormous jaws, positioning it perfectly beside the last. It was an amazing performance, but Sadie had no time for awe.

"I need your help," she said, speaking very hurriedly in her desire to find someone else to share the burden of responsibility. "You know Phoebe—the Princess—she's been taken captive."

"That is terrible news," Xpql agreed, lovingly rolling the stone into a precise juxtaposition with those around it.

Sadie stared at him. "Yes, it is terrible!" she said. "It's awful! It's outrageous! What are we going to do about it?"

"Storm the Glass Castle, I suppose," said the Dragon, heading to the back of the cave to select the next rock.

"Then why are you still doing that? We don't have time for this!"

The Dragon stopped. "It is my time for bower making," he explained. "My blood demands it—and, as we say, 'To go against blood is to freeze water with fire.' It is an undeniable demand, the demand of blood."

"That's ridiculous," Sadie objected. "Part of being human and not an animal is the ability to control your urges."

"Perhaps," Xpql answered maddeningly. She had only known him three minutes, and already she hated him. "I would not know—I am not a human." He let out a little snort of gray-tinged white smoke and went back to making his spiral. "But I know this: when we enter Graysmoke, there is no time to waste. If we waited until our fires grew bright, there would be no more eggs to bring hope to my People—the eggs would be quite cooked." Then he stopped. "Forgive me," he said, understanding dawning in his gold eyes, "what you said about humans—now I understand. You must be the Princess's foster sister."

"I'm not her *foster* sister," Sadie replied indignantly. "I'm her *real* sister, and don't you forget it!"

"As you wish," said the Dragon with a shrug. "But among my People we have a saying that 'blood is thicker than water,' and it is my blood, not yours, that flows through her veins, May Fire and Water Protect Them. The Princess Xthpqltthpqlwxn is my sister."

"Well," said Sadie, growing decidedly hot, "we have sayings, too, where I come from, and if I knew them all, I'm sure I could prove to you that family is stronger than blood. Phoebe grew up with me—trusted me—*loved* me, and I love her. I'm her *real* sister and she is mine."

The Dragon bent down to pick up another rock. Moving it to the end of the spiral, he let out a self-satisfied snort of smoke before turning back to Sadie.

"You are just as my grandmother said," he pronounced. "She always said you had the courage of your convictions."

He said this like it was a bad thing, and Sadie felt an intense dislike for him and his supercilious attitudes. But then, with a pang, she realized that he was the closest thing she had to an ally in all that strange and desolate land—and an ally, treated properly, may become a friend. She sighed. If only Mrs. Fitz Edna were there, it would have been so much easier.

"I wish your grandmother were here," she whispered.

"Where is my grandmother?" Xpql inquired, turning his attention to a pile of bluish stones. He proceeded to place them meticulously between each of the rocks in the spiral.

"I forgot that you didn't know," Sadie answered reluctantly. "She is dead. The Barbazion killed her."

There was a long unhappy silence.

"We have a saying," Xpql said at last. "'The young long for fire, but the old ones long for extinguishing.' Perhaps she is glad to be rid of the fire now."

He hung his head. For a moment, the cave was very loud with the silence of their grief.

Sadie must have slept, for when she woke, Xpql was standing at the edge of the cave. Even without seeing his face, Sadie could guess the mournful expression on it.

"What's wrong?" she asked.

"I have given the call," he answered. "The bower is ready, but no female has answered my call."

"Perhaps there are none nearby," Sadie said, to soothe him.

"But that is not possible," Xpql replied. "All of my People come here from Xthltg when the first gray smoke comes from their nostrils. I cannot be alone."

"But Xpql," said Sadie, wishing she did not have to give this dreadful news as well, "didn't you hear? The Barbazion . . . Xthltg . . . the river . . ."

"What are you saying?" Xpql asked in a terrible voice, and Sadie found she was saying nothing at all. She could not make her mouth tell him about the destruction of his home.

"It is as I feared," Xpql mourned when she finally told him about Xthltg. "When I first arrived here and began my bower, the slopes were crawling with my People, but now I am alone. And I am more than alone, for you tell me I will be alone even if I return home."

He hung his head then, but Sadie didn't want to see him mourn. She wanted to see him angry, as angry as she was, so that their anger could carry them safely across the dangers that faced them.

"Then we can be alone together!" she cried, leaping up and putting her hand onto the Dragon's withers. "We can work together, you and I. We will rescue my sister—*our* sister—and then we will have justice! Your grandmother said that Phoebe was the key . . . once we have her back, we will make the Barbazion pay for what they did to Xthltg, what they've done to your People! We will destroy them!"

"Destroy the Barbazion?" the Dragon said, lifting his head. "Your humans are more foolhardy than I thought. How will we even reach the Glass Castle? I am still a Graysmoke and cannot yet fly, and you look as if you can hardly walk. Besides, how could the two of us destroy them? They are monsters, and they are numerous, and we are merely us, and we are few."

"We *can*," Sadie declared. "We have a saying where I come from, up in the halls in my school. It says, 'Never doubt that a small group of thoughtful, committed citizens can change the world; indeed, it's the only thing that ever has.'"

"What does that mean?" asked Xpql.

"It means we leave in the morning," said Sadie decidedly. "It means we move against the Barbazion as soon as they sleep."

8

The Flight down the Mountain

Not long after the sun came up on the deserted mountain, Xpql boiled a few fish in the steaming pools for their breakfast. Then they set their faces towards the distant Glass Castle, trudging down the mountain face away from Xthltg. They did not make quick progress. Xpql walked very slowly in his awkward lizard's gait, plodding along with great force and effort. He laid down each foot with ponderous precision, as if waiting for the slight reverberation of the ground to fade away before preparing for the next step, and it drove Sadie crazy.

"This would be a lot easier if you could just fly us off the mountain," Sadie pointed out.

Xpql let out a plume of gray-tinged smoke in answer and waddled ahead with great reptilian dignity.

At least it was a beautiful morning. The evergreen trees were fragrant and lovely, the little rivulets silver in the morning light, and once more the mountainside was covered with a thick blanket of mist, swirling in little eddies like the smoke that came from Xpql's widespread nostrils.

The sight of all that beauty seemed to have a mellowing effect upon the Dragon. "We have a saying," he told Sadie confidentially. "We say that the mountain is like the greatest of all hatchlings, pouring her first smoke out over the land. This is a very sacred place, this mountain, and these pools are the most sacred of all—you should feel honored to tread here, human."

"My name is Sadie," Sadie interrupted, but the Dragon went on.

"We have another saying, too: 'The mountain watches over the eggs as a mothering bird does.' And in turn, we from the eggs will watch over the mountain. That is the way of things. I have always hoped to serve my time as guardian of the mountain, to protect it against the Barbazion. . . ."

Some of the melancholy from the night had settled back upon him. "But perhaps I was born too late—perhaps my time has passed before it even arrived. I suspect the Barbazion have killed every one of the guards in the watchtowers. The silence last night told me."

Sadie could not get him to speak after that. His melancholy seemed impenetrable. Sadie felt her own mood deteriorate in his gloom; even the mountain seemed affected. The thick fog was no longer so pearly as it had been in the morning. It seemed yellowed and sickly, and it did not burn away under the heat of noon as it had done the day before. Sadie's eyes began to smart, and she found it harder to breathe even though they walked at such a glacial speed. It was as maddening as walking with Phoebe on those interminable strolls when she had to stop and examine every bug and snail, scowling when anyone tried to get her to hurry along.

"Can't you go any quicker?" she asked Xpql impatiently.

The Dragon drew himself up and looked at Sadie with great dignity. "We have a saying," he replied stuffily. "'The egg rolls quickly down the slope, but knows not where it goes.'"

"We have a saying, too," Sadie retorted. "It goes like this: 'Move it or lose it.' Come on, Xpql! Walking with you is like walking with my sister, and *snails* can outpace her—I know that for a fact." But thinking of Phoebe had been a mistake: it made her feel sick and desperate.

"Do not speak so disrespectfully of *my* sister," Xpql sniffed. "My people do not take her examinations so lightly—we think it is an honor to watch her learn from the world. Although she has a strange form, her heart is wise, and her mind is loving. There is much she knows, for she speaks to all creatures who will listen, and listens to all that will talk."

"She does?" asked Sadie.

"She does," Xpql confirmed. "And like my sister, I will take my time. In any case, I don't know why you wish to hurry. Very likely it is our deaths to which you hurry us along."

Sadie was about to give a pert reply when they turned the corner of the path. With horror she saw that Xpql might very well be correct. The bottom of the mountain was on fire.

They stared at the fire in disbelief. Rivers of flame were climbing up the mountain's sides like a column of advancing soldiers, and a thick black smoke hung over the land like a pall.

"Look at it," said Sadie—unnecessarily, for Xpql could do nothing but stare down at the flames. "It's not a *wild* fire—I mean, not originally. Look at it how it's all evenly spaced around the bottom of the mountain. This wasn't an accident."

"No," Xpql agreed. "The Barbazion have moved on us again. The guards must be dead down there, just as I thought."

Sadie's eyes stung, whether from smoke or tears, and the rage boiled within her again. The cruelty of the Barbazion was so complete that it kindled a desperate fury in her chest. Fire and water were supposed to protect the Dragons, but the Barbazion had used both against their sacred places. It brought the thirst for justice upon her again, and she longed to hit something. "How dare they!" she erupted, pointing down at the ugly black smoke. "I *hate* them! I *hate* them!" She felt a little guilty then, thinking how her mother always told her it was wrong to hate. But there was no getting around it—she *did* hate the Barbazion, and the force of her hatred blazed within her, driving out even her fear.

"I will *destroy* them!" she thundered. "When we get down there, I'm going to tear them apart, limb from limb!"

Xpql appraised her cautiously. "I doubt if you will have that opportunity," he pointed out. "I don't see how you think you are going to get through that fire."

"Are you sure you can't fly yet?" Sadie demanded.

"No," he sighed. "No, it seems it will be our lot to die up here alone, without our revenge."

But Sadie would not be daunted. Mrs. Fitz Edna had always said Sadie's outrage was one of her great strengths, and it appeared she was right. She looked down the burning slope of the mountain and didn't see the danger. Instead, her fiery eye saw the moment she would bring the Barbazion to their knees to account for the suffering they had caused the Dragons, to pay for the destruction they had wrought, and, most of all, to force them to return Phoebe to her family. And then, staring down through the smoke into her visions of revenge, Sadie saw the road that would carry them to safety: the silver river, burnished to a dull sheen by the smoke.

"We'll ride the river," she announced. "We just need to make some sort of a raft."

It is of course a tricky proposition to construct a raft, even when you are not faced with the suboptimal conditions of being ropeless, toolless, and without experience in the path of a raging forest fire. Sadie's first attempt, and her second, were decided failures. Determinedly, she set to work on a third, but patience had long since boiled away under the force of her righteous anger, and in the end she threw away the insufficient sticks and twigs she had gathered and scowled at her companion.

"Can't you just fly us off this heap?" she snapped.

"No," Xpql answered. "Can you?"

They continued to work in silence. In the end, they managed to weave together a little mat wide enough to keep their heads and shoulders out of the waters.

"We will ride this thing to our deaths, you know," Xpql predicted gloomily, but Sadie faced the river with grim determination and launched them into the current.

At first their progress was maddeningly slow. The river seemed to pay no attention to their hurry, but dawdled and dallied, minced and meandered, and before long Sadie began to feel not only angry, but ridiculous. Here they were, drifting lazily down a brook as if whiling away a summer's afternoon! Here they were, sauntering through a picturesque alpine scene, as if they were not facing a fiery inferno! But now and again the slope of the mountain grew steeper, and the green waters became flecked with white, and once or twice they passed over little rapids that left Sadie breathless.

They were getting closer to the vanguard of the fire. Just

up ahead, a great sheet of crimson flame rose above the trees. The trunks looked black against the red light, and here and there a tree was outlined in vivid yellow flame.

And then, as they drew close, the heat hit them like a wall. Even the waters of the river began to feel warm against Sadie's legs, and she felt her nails lifting slightly from her fingers, the way it feels when you put your hand inside an oven to feel if it's hot enough for biscuits. She kept her face close to the skimming surface of the water and sought some coolness there as she tried to imagine she was merely rafting with Phoebe on a pleasant family vacation—but it was impossible with Xpql's doleful sighs of resignation beside her. At last he laid a gentle claw on her shoulder.

"There it is," he said softly. "They say each person knows when he looks upon his own death, and there is ours." Sadie lifted her eyes from the mat and looked. A sheet of fire stretched across the river, and they were hurtling straight for it.

"How—" Sadie began, but it didn't seem worth it to waste her breath wondering how her plan had gone so terribly awry. She wondered wildly whether they could swim under the curtain of fire, or if she could possibly get to the banks before they reached it, and then, unhappily, she wondered whether she would choke to death on the smoke before she felt the searing of the flames.

It was very strange, as she hurtled towards her death, how slowly the seconds seemed to pass. It was as if someone knew she needed more time. She no longer felt the warm water of the river on her body, or the sharp edges of the raft under her chest. Instead she felt that she was floating over the scene, making plans that would never succeed, and writing the last letters to those she loved. She thought of her parents, and ached for them, knowing that they would never know the outrageous fates of their two daughters; she thought of Picker, who would never know that Sadie had at last trusted in the impossible and lived out an adventure clearly intended for another. Mostly she thought of Phoebe, with her enormous gold eyes fastened fiercely on whatever she looked upon, drinking in people and things as if learning them by heart, and her heart ached some more.

Then suddenly she was back in the river. The waters around her were not just warm, but almost painfully hot; the very air felt like fire, flecked with ash. The wall of flame rose up above them, striped with bands of heat, the red flickering at the top above the glowing yellow, and the blinding white at the bottom. Sadie could not take her eyes off it: the beauty and horror of it were too much. The crackling and the moaning and groaning of the trees was deafening—in a moment, they would be upon it.

"Tell Phoebe . . ." she said desperately, to Xpql, to the wind, to the fates, to anyone who would listen—but there was no time to finish the thought, for suddenly the wall of fire seemed to part in front of their eyes. Sadie gaped: the river was swinging around a bend, and they were shooting triumphantly between the walls of fire on both banks. And then Sadie and Xpql saw a welcome sight: they had made it down the mountain, and the river was carrying them down to the plain that spread out before them like the promise of safety.

9

In Which Things Only Get Worse

Sodden, stiff, and bedraggled, they hauled themselves out of the river and gazed over the flat landscape. It was desolate, desertlike, and dreary, and Sadie saw that the only reason the fire wasn't raging there, too, was that there was nothing there to burn. The plain was as lifeless as the moon, and once more Sadie felt how very alone they were in the middle of that wide wasteland, and how vulnerable.

Xpql wasn't even looking out over the desert. He was staring at the smoking ruins far to the left and right of the river.

"Those were the towers that guarded our sacred mountain," he said. "Now I know it is true. The Barbazion have won. They have destroyed everything I've ever known and loved. There is nothing left to fight for." He closed his mournful eyes and sank to the ground.

"You can't give up now!" Sadie cried out. "Your grandmother always said that where there's life there's hope, and you and I are still alive—and so's my sister." She swallowed hard, hoping it was true. Again she had a flash of the little figure in the tower, round eyes staring, looking for help, the way she'd looked when she'd gotten her head stuck between the bars of the park fence. Sadie took a deep breath, and armed herself with fury.

"My sister is the key—your grandmother said so. Once we get her back, the Dragons will be able to defeat the Barbazion once and for all, and *this* will never happen again! Get up, Xpql! If you just lie there, well, then, you're letting the Barbazion win!"

"My grandmother always said you were tenacious," Xpql grumbled, "although she spoke of it as if it were a good quality." He sighed again. "If you insist, we go on, though I doubt we will succeed."

"We *will*," promised Sadie grimly. "Which way do we go? Do we follow the river?"

"That's as good a plan as any—" Xpql answered, "unless you're trying to get to the Glass Castle."

"Fine," Sadie groaned. "Tell me which way we *should* go."

They left the river. It was not an inviting scene before them. The sparse grass was more gray than green, and it grew in lumpy clumps that made a straight path impossible to find. The ground itself was harsh on the feet. The little hills and hummocks were pockmarked by outthrusts of lava, and bits of sharp obsidian were scattered on the ground.

"It looks like glass," said Sadie, turning over a piece between her fingers.

"Put it down," Xpql ordered. "We never touch the black glass—only the Barbazion make use of it. Put it down now, human."

"My name is Sadie," said Sadie meekly, but she dropped the obsidian as he'd asked.

They continued across the sullen plains. There was no life to be seen at all, except a few more of the land starfish, gray and fleshy.

"Do not try to eat those," Xpql warned Sadie, with the voice of one with an unhappy experience. "They taste most unpleasant and turn your excretions orange."

"I was just wondering if we could talk to them and ask them if they've seen the Barbazion," Sadie answered. "I mean, since we can talk to the animals."

"Just because we can talk to them does not mean they will answer," Xpql replied. "These are the sort of creature only my sister would have the patience to talk to. If we had a week, perhaps, we could find out this one's name; in two months, we might know if any creature had come close enough to step upon it. No, human, we will get no information from this quarter."

He waddled away, dismissing Sadie and her idea. "My name is Sadie," she called after him, and then she, too, continued walking in the vague direction of the Glass Castle.

It was an exhausting march. Sadie had to check her gait constantly to make sure she did not shoot off ahead of the Dragon. Her feet hurt. The grit and grime of her three days in Dragonland were rubbing raw places on her sore feet, and she had at least three new blisters. And it wasn't just her feet—everything hurt. Her lungs hurt; her legs hurt—even her hair seemed to hurt. She sighed. The plains stretched out in front of them, infinite and uninviting. There were a thousand reasons to be discouraged, but Sadie tried to think of what Mrs. Fitz Edna would say in this situation.

"At least the Barbazion can't ambush us," she said, kicking at a hunk of lava and discovering painfully that it was still attached to the ground. "We'd see them coming, in this flat landscape."

"Yes," agreed Xpql. "We will watch them come to slaughter us, with nowhere to go."

"*Ay, caramba,*" said Sadie to the heavens. "Could you just lighten up for a moment? Your grandmother said a one-legged creature would be happy for three legs to walk on. Isn't that true?"

Xpql nodded his head in agreement. "Yes," he concurred. "I would be glad for three legs in this situation." And so they continued on their gloomy way.

It was hot—desert hot. There was nothing beautiful at all to break the drabness. Even the interesting second sun in the yellow sky was obscured by the smoke that still drifted from the mountain behind them. But Xpql's eyes were better than Sadie's. "Look," he said, pointing to a shadow on the horizon. "There is one of my People's strongholds. We should head in that direction, although I doubt we will find anyone alive."

The suns were low in the sky before they reached the tower. As soon as Sadie saw it, she saw that Xpql's pessimism had not been unwarranted. The iron gates that guarded the doors had been battered in. They hung crookedly on their hinges, bent in the middle like a person who recoils from a blow. Sadie could feel the emptiness behind them, a palpable loneliness that came down the stone stairs of the tower.

"We should go up," said Xpql reluctantly. "We should make sure we will find no help here, or that we cannot offer any in turn."

"No—" Sadie stammered. "I don't think I can stand it. . . ."

But Xpql was already making his lugubrious way up the stairs. Torn between the shared dangers of the tower and the lonely vulnerability there on the plains, Sadie hurried after him.

She found him standing over a body at the landing. It had once been a young Dragon, but all the life was gone from her. Xpql hung his head.

"I knew this one," he said. "It was Rsmgt, and she might have led us all one day—that was what they said. And now . . ." Sadie stared down, her eyes filled with tears, even though she had never seen this Rsmgt in life.

They found the others up the second flight of stairs. They had obviously fought valiantly, for the walls were covered with scorch marks, and the blood on the ground was a bluish silver Xpql said belonged to the Barbazion.

"Ten," Xpql counted. "Ten more who will never again spread their limbs and feel the rush of fire propelling them forward; ten who will never again sing the songs of triumph. There are now ten widows and widowers, uncounted orphans; ten mothers and ten fathers who have lost the best parts of themselves. It is an evil thing that has happened here."

Sadie looked down at the bodies. She had never seen a corpse before. It was amazing how lifeless they looked. They did not look at all like they were sleeping. They looked erased.

"Xpql," she whispered, "the flies . . . shouldn't we brush away the flies?" The insects were thick around the eyes and mouths of the dead.

"Why bother?" Xpql asked. "There is nothing here. They are gone. There is nothing more we can do for them—and I doubt there is anything more we can do for any of us."

"Don't *say* that!" Sadie cried. "You *can't* let the Barbazion win."

"It's not a matter of letting," Xpql replied. "The Barbazion have a way of winning all on their own."

But Sadie looked around and saw the bodies sprawled on the ground and refused to believe it. "*We're* still alive," she reminded him, "so we're going. Come on, Xpql. We *will* rescue my sister, and then the Dragons—your People—will triumph. I promise!" She said this with much more conviction than she felt, but it felt good to have someone saying those words. "We *will* rescue her," she repeated.

Night was falling quickly. When they came out of the dark of the tower, it was hardly lighter outside.

"The Barbazion will be out soon," Xpql observed. "They will find us here, but they will find us out there as well. Shall we go or stay? It is all the same to me where I die."

"Well, come on, then," said Sadie grimly. "Let's die closer to our goal. Then we can feel like we've accomplished something."

They marched on. Even their short rest in the tower had reminded Sadie's sore body how very tired she was. She was remembering a time the summer before when their mother had let Sadie take Phoebe to the corner store for a Popsicle. Sadie had been walking ahead of her dawdling sister, and she hadn't seen when Phoebe fell. By the time she turned around, Phoebe had scraped both knees and one elbow, and was sitting on the ground with a very serious look on her face. Sadie had struggled to carry her sister home. She had made it only two blocks before she had to put her sister down: Phoebe was very heavy. Now Sadie felt that weight crushing her down again, but it was the weight of responsibility without the rewarding pressure of Phoebe's hot face against her cheek.

"Poor Phoebe!" she said now. "Can you imagine her, alone in that tower, in *jail*? And she's so shy. . . ."

"Shy!" Xpql echoed scornfully. "The Princess is not *shy*. I have heard her many times, surrounded by dozens of her followers, telling us amazing stories about Humanland. She was never shy."

"How do you know?" Sadie retorted. "I saw her *every day*, and I saw how she wanted me to hold her hand when she went to kindergarten, and how she needed me— Hey! Where are you going?"

From the proud cast of his head, she saw she had offended him.

"Xpql," she amended cautiously, "Xpql, I'm sorry. I didn't mean that you didn't know my sister. I guess we have a lot to learn about her from each other."

Xpql walked on, but he might have been somewhat appeased.

The moon rose, and still they walked on, each alone with their thoughts. Sadie was exhausted. At last she saw, impossibly, that she was falling behind him. She remembered with longing how it had felt to ride on Mrs. Fitz Edna, and looked wistfully at Xpql's broad back. But Xpql, catching her look, drew back with visible disgust.

"I would offer to carry you—" he said, very seriously, "—*if* I were a pack animal. But the People are not beasts of burden. Remember that, human."

"My name is Sadie," said Sadie in a very small voice.

They walked on in silence.

At last Xpql started over in a more conciliatory tone. "I am not offended, human," he said. "It is just that I cannot forget the stories of how the Barbazion treat my People. I know some who flew near the Glass Castle. They said they saw our People there, captured, blindered, made to carry bits between their teeth. . . . But why should we be surprised, when they enslave even the unicorns? Imagine, unicorns, forced to pull a carriage for the pleasure of the Barbazion! The unicorns, who should live free in their meadows, eating the starflowers and moongrass! It is disgusting."

They continued to walk. In the strange shadows of the moonlight, the desert seemed more pointy and inhospitable than ever. Then Sadie looked up and saw something fly across the disk of the moon.

"Xpql!" she cried. "What *is* that!"

She saw a flash of fear behind the pessimistic resignation in his eyes as he turned his face to the sky. Then his tense shoulders relaxed.

"It is one of the Winged Ones," he said. "They are the last of the free creatures on this world. They are wild, their own creatures, and they fly where they wish, as my People once did. Not even the Barbazion would attempt to tame them."

Sadie stared: the distant creature wheeled about, as if galloping in the sky. "They're beautiful," she breathed. She was glad she had seen such a sight, and she felt some strange tie to Xpql that she had seen it with him. She stared back up at the creature. For the first time, she felt some of the wonder Phoebe had tried to express about Dragonland as she sat at the kitchen table and spun out tales that no one heard. The familiar lump grew in her throat as she thought of her sister. "It feels like a good omen, doesn't it?" she asked hopefully.

Xpql let out a gloomy puff of smoke. "My People have a saying—" he began, but Sadie interrupted him.

"Don't say anything," she said, but not without affection. "*I* think it's a good omen, and I can't stand another one of your pessimistic clichés right now."

"I ask you not to disparage the wisdom of my People," Xpql answered, a little stuffily, and he walked ahead with a proud swing of his tail. And then, suddenly, he was gone.

10

Under the Ground

Sadie stared in astonishment at the place where Xpql had been. There was a blackness on the ground, in the midst of all the darkness, and Sadie saw it was a great hole. She peered down into it.

"Xpql! Are you there? Are you all right?"

Sounds of scratching, and small stones skittering down.

"This is it, then," came Xpql's gloomy voice from down below. "I have escaped fire only to die in a hole. Good-bye, human."

"My name is Sadie," Sadie answered impatiently. "Wait— I'm going to try to get you out."

"Wait," Xpql repeated. "Yes, I shall wait. That is all I can do in this hole—wait for death."

"Are you sure you can't fly yet?" Sadie asked, but Xpql answered her only with an offended silence.

In the dim light of the gibbous moon, Sadie looked around for a rope, a pole, a tree—anything to help him, but unless she was going to throw down enough pieces of rock to let Xpql climb out, there was nothing there of any use—except of course, Sadie herself.

"Xpql," she called, trying to gauge the distance down to the dim red lights that were the Dragon's eyes. "I'm coming down. . . ."

Her mother always said that she leapt before she looked. "*Think* before you commit yourself," she always urged Sadie, and those words rang in Sadie's ears too late as she fell into the hole.

"Well, human," said Xpql, when she'd landed, "I have to say I don't think much of your plan. Now we are both trapped."

"My name is Sadie, and you're welcome," Sadie retorted. "Now let's work on getting you out of here."

"Get me out of here?" the Dragon repeated gloomily. "There is no way out of here at all, except through the passageway whose name is Death."

Sadie was about to object when she realized he might very well be right. As she looked up to the dark window of sky, she saw that the hole was much too deep for them to escape. It was twelve or fifteen feet from the bottom of the hole up to the surface, and jumping in to save the Dragon was decidedly the stupidest, most shortsighted thing Sadie had ever done.

The light from Xpql's eyes was getting brighter. They had been sitting, side by side, contemplating their plight, when Sadie caught sight of something in their red beams. She stood up and began creeping into the darkness.

"Xpql," she said, "I think—I think this isn't a hole at all! I think it's a cave."

It certainly seemed to be a cave. Sadie wandered farther into the darkness, her fingers brushing against the ropy texture of the walls. The walls were smooth and dry, and the floor and ceiling free of stalagmites and stalactites, but the hole was most certainly cavelike. Sadie didn't know it, but they had fallen into a lava tube cave, formed back when the flat-topped mountain had first hurled ash and lava all over the plain. As the lava had run down the mountain's side, it cooled, and as it cooled, it formed a rock shell, but the lava inside the shell continued to flow, leaving a catacomb layer of intersecting caves beneath the surface. Over the millennia those caves had been entirely covered by dirt: a secret lost to sentient beings who think their own lives are long.

"Come on," Sadie said to Xpql, pointing her face towards the deeper darkness of the tunnel. "Here it is—our way out."

"Why bother?" Xpql sighed. "We might as well die here as anywhere else."

"Why not bother?" Sadie returned. "We might as well die anywhere else as here."

It was slow going, walking in that branching network of caves with only the dim red light from Xpql's eyes to guide them. It was also getting very cold—not just the chill of the desert night, but a deeper cold, like the cold of ice. Not for the first time, Sadie wished she were wearing something other than her pajamas and battered sneakers over her sore bare feet.

"Of course," she said scientifically, mostly to distract herself from the unpleasant sensation of freezing, "cold air is heavier than hot. Once the cold air got down here, any warm air from above wouldn't be able move the cold out. I bet there could even be *ice* down here. There are ice caves on Earth—my father told Phoebe and me about them."

"If there is ice down here, we will never be able to share the story of it with anyone," Xpql sighed. "This passage is heading down. We will never see the world of light again."

It was true, but Sadie was tired of his pessimism. She was just about to start complaining about Xpql's constant continuo of gloom when her foot stepped out onto a patch of ice. For an infinite second, she tried to regain her balance, but before she could draw a breath, both feet shot out from under her. Then she was skittering down what seemed like an interminable sheet of ice, ricocheting painfully off jagged pieces of lava that studded the way down, until at last she landed bruised and breathless at the bottom.

"There's no time for this," Xpql reprimanded from up above. His voice sounded very far away, and when Sadie looked back up the way she had fallen, the two red lights of his eyes shone like pinpricks.

"Sorry," she called up sarcastically, feeling for broken bones. "But don't worry about me—I put ice on it right away."

Rubbing her sore arms and legs (and most especially her bruised backside), Sadie stood up and tried to walk back up the ice slide, sliding right back down again for her trouble. She tried again, once, then twice, but there was no helping it. It was simply too hard to climb up a sheet of ice in the dark, and her frustration suddenly gave way to fear.

"It's no use," she called up to the Dragon. "Either you'll have to go on without me, or you'll have to join me down here."

An audible sigh from above. "I really think it would have been better to stay together," he remarked.

"I agree," Sadie sighed. She looked back up at the sheet of ice and the weight of her loneliness fell down upon her. It had been such a stupid little thing, to slip and fall like that, and now she was going to die all alone in the dark. Phoebe was going to stay a prisoner of the Barbazion, and all the Dragons would be slaughtered, all because of a stupid mistake. It wasn't fair! Phoebe was only five, and shouldn't be locked in a room far away from those who loved her. *I'm so sorry, Phoebe,* she whispered. *I tried—I really tried. And I'm sorry, Mom, Dad—I know you trusted me.*

A whiff of sulfur and a grunt from above. And then Sadie barely had time to move out of the way before the Dragon came thundering down.

"What did you do that for?" Sadie asked him incredulously as he landed beside her.

"Well," he sniffed, gingerly picking himself up from the ground. "As I said, it is better for us to stick together." He sniffed again, and looked around, the red light from his eyes shining on the ice. "I can only hope there is another way out of here," he said, shaking his heavy head, "or we will freeze to death, as well as starve."

"I hear it's an easy death," Sadie said, rolling her eyes, but she was in truth relieved that he had joined her down there in the dark.

They crept on, more slowly this time because Sadie tested every step twice to make sure she would not fall again. She walked with one hand on Xpql's shoulder so she could share the small light that came from his eyes, and the Dragon stood by patiently every time she picked herself up after a fall. At last he spoke to her gruffly.

"Get on my back," he ordered.

"What?"

"Just get on my back. I can use my claws to keep from slipping—you cannot. You should ride."

"But I thought . . ."

"*Please,* human," he said, his eyes glowing brighter. "I do not like to see you fall."

"Oh," said Sadie. "Oh. Well, thank you. And my name is Sadie."

She climbed up onto his back and he started forward, swishing his hips and shoulders in his slow, splay-limbed lizard's gait. It was very different from riding a horse, much harder to keep her seat, so she leaned forward and held the Dragon around the neck in a loose embrace. Strangely, it made her feel more kindly towards him. Xpql, too, seemed to feel the change, for he grunted a little and tried to shift his back to make her more comfortable. For the first time, Sadie found a little solace that he was there, and she was glad she was not entirely alone in an ice cave on a strange planet a zillion miles, at least, from home and family. Except (she thought) in a way, Xpql *was* her family—they were both brother and sister to Phoebe. *We're almost like cousins,* she thought. *And I loved Mrs. Fitz Edna like a grandmother, just like he did.*

She was about to say some of this to Xpql when she heard his breath come out of his mouth with a great rush.

"Look," he breathed.

Sadie strained her eyes and saw what had stopped him short. It was a great river flowing in front of them, roiling and foaming and tossing up spray, but it was frozen, as if it had been stopped in time. Sadie stared. It was so strange and beautiful and achingly sad that those waves would never break on distant rocky shores that Sadie felt she could say nothing at all. She wished she could see the river in the sunshine, see the light glint off the green ice, see the places where the foam crystals sparkled in little eddies, but at the same time, she realized that if the sun shone down on it, it would all melt away back into ordinary water. She knew then that here was a sight not meant to be seen by any eyes.

"It was just here, all the time, in the dark, and nobody saw it," she wondered.

"We are seeing it now," Xpql whispered back. And then: "I'm so glad we're seeing it now."

They continued up the river, slowly, so that they could stare at the wonderful ice. They wandered there, taking it all in, marveling at the stillness of this most beautiful place so far under the ground. They passed by icicle stalactites and fantastic ice stalagmites until at last they came to the headwaters. There they could see how the water had entered the cave: up above them, tunnel upon tunnel had collapsed under the weight of the water, leaving a single enormous cavern, vaulted like a cathedral. The water had once poured over the edge from another tunnel, far above them, falling in a great crashing waterfall into the caverns below. Over the generations, the cold had stopped it in its tracks, and now each drop stood frozen in time, a silent, still cataract, and neither Sadie nor Xpql could do anything but stare.

"We should climb up," Sadie said reluctantly. "That's the way out."

"I know," said Xpql. "I know we must leave, but I don't want to go. When we leave here, we will never see all this again. And here, for the first time, I feel that what we do at the surface does not matter at all. For the first time since I understood about the Prophecy, I feel quite serene."

They sat there for a long time, not talking, just looking at the ice. Then Sadie saw with surprise that something was moving. It was a drop of water, a little one, newly freed from the ice, rolling lazily down the frozen torrents of the waterfall.

"Look," she said, pointing, and Xpql's breath came out of his nostrils with a thick rush of smoke. Two more drops followed the first.

"What's happening?" Sadie asked, her heart skipping a little with fear. But Xpql merely sighed again. "It is I," he said. "I cannot stay here. I have found the most beautiful place of all, a place where none of my sorrows matter, and if I stay, I will destroy it." He sighed again, and a little puff of smoke rolled over towards the frothy waves and set them to melting too.

"Oh," said Sadie. "Your smoke. I understand."

"Let us go now, then," Xpql urged unhappily. "I do not want to hurt this place. Let us go now."

They began climbing up the sides of the waterfall, Sadie first so that Xpql could catch her if she fell. It was painful work, finding the sharp handholds and footholds, hauling themselves up inch by inch, ignoring the scrapes and scratches. It took a long time, and Sadie was very cold. The cold seemed more intense, more vicious, the more tired she became. Her hands began to ache with it, and she was sure they were turning blue. When they reached the first upper cave, she jumped around with her hands in the armpits of the tattered pajamas to warm them, but they hurt so badly she was not sure if she would be able to climb anymore. Xpql watched her with concern.

"Human," he said finally, "Sadie-Human, come over here." Then, gruffly, gently, he blew on her hands to warm them, first just a little warm smoke, and then hotter, and Sadie almost cried in gratitude.

"You are exhausted," he said at last. "Let us rest here; tomorrow we will find the way out."

"I can't sleep," Sadie moaned through chattering teeth, though she wanted nothing more than to lie down and rest. "If you fall asleep in the cold, you f-f-freeze to death—and this is certainly c-c-old. . . ."

"Sleep," Xpql repeated, pulling her close to his hot body. "I will help you." And then, taking a deep breath, he blew a bubble of smoke around her, as Mrs. Fitz Edna had done on their flight from Earth. In that bubble, warmed by her own breath, Sadie slept.

11

In the Catacombs

When she woke, Xpql was melting some ice in a cup-shaped piece of lava, and so they had lava tea for breakfast.

"You know," he said, "I was thinking that it is not so strange after all for me to be in this cold, dark place. This is my Mountain Time—the time before Blacksmoke when my people learn to confront their fears alone. Of course, this Mountain is under the ground, and I am not alone. . . ." He paused. "I am glad I am not alone, Sadie-Human. I find when you talk, the cold is not quite so bitter. Talk to me. Tell me about my sister."

"*My* sister," Sadie corrected. "What can I tell you about Phoebe? Well, for starters, you would not believe the imagination on that child. The stories she told about Dragonland . . ."

She paused. "Of course, maybe she's not so imaginative after all—everything she told us seems to be true."

Suddenly she started to laugh.

"You know," she said to Xpql, "a lot of things are starting to make sense. Like when she learned how to crawl, she did it with her arms and legs to the side instead of under her—like the way you walk. Your grandmother had to get down on her hands and knees and show Phoebe how it was done. She was teaching Phoebe to be a better human baby, I guess, like she had to teach her not to drink Tabasco sauce out of the bottle. And I guess it does explain the asthma. But oh, Xpql! She may be a Dragon, but she is most definitely my sister."

She laughed heartily then, for the first time since she had set foot in Dragonland. It was a great relief, laughing. The weight of their quest fell away from her for a moment, and she felt generous.

"And you?" she asked. "Will *you* tell *me* a story about my sister?"

Xpql paused and considered, and then he spoke. "*My* sister is unique," he said. "She does not look like us, but her heart is of the People. More than once I have seen her stare down a creature more than twice her size—"

"She growls at dogs back home," Sadie interrupted. Then she laughed again. "Of course, she was probably just talking to them!"

Xpql nodded. "Just so. We can all speak to the animals, of

course, but not all of us know what to say. The Princess knows because she listens. She is a deep one, for one so young. My grandmother always said that she was born with both eyes open, and both ears to the ground. My sister does not waste time. Every moment she is learning and thinking."

"She's awfully stubborn," Sadie countered, as if subconsciously trying to show that by knowing Phoebe's faults, she knew her sister better.

"She is *determined*," corrected Xpql. "If she has a fault, it is that she is too gullible. I have seen her stride right up to a walking whale and offer to share a meal with it, without any thought of the consequence of its big sharp teeth."

"She isn't *gullible*," Sadie objected, "she's *trusting*. She loves people and animals, and they make her happy. But she is awfully literal."

"She's not *literal*, she's precise. But she is noisy."

"She's not noisy, she's exuberant!"

"She *is* exuberant," repeated Xpql. "She is exuberant, and we all love her for it. I do hope the Barbazion have not taken that from her."

They both fell silent then.

"Do you think she's still . . . all right?" Sadie asked at last.

Xpql considered. "According to the Prophecy, the army who holds the Princess will be invincible. I do not believe that the Barbazion would hurt such a weapon once it was in their possession." He paused. "Of course," he continued, "I am often wrong."

The two of them sat there, both thinking about their sister, when suddenly Xpql hissed, "Sadie-Human . . ."

Sadie barely heard him. She was still thinking about Phoebe's sweet, funny face, with the mouth that was always talking and the gold eyes that were always looking.

"Sadie-Human!"

Now Phoebe's growly voice was in her ears, and she did not want Xpql to interrupt.

"SADIE-HUMAN!"

She could not ignore the note of panic in his voice.

"What? Xpql, what's wrong?"

"Many things are wrong," Xpql responded. "But the new thing that is wrong is that we are not the first to have come this way."

He pointed. There, screwed into the rock of the wall, was a bracket, and in the bracket was a piece of burned wood.

"A torch," Sadie breathed. "What is this place? And what is *that?*"

That was a painting—an enormous painting. Sadie stared, and crept forward for a closer look. Then she recoiled in horror.

The painting showed a monster—a hideous, malevolent monster. It had a cruel, curved beak and a ring of eyes that went all around its head, and it wore a necklace of Dragon skulls around its neck. Its long whiplike tail was wrapped around the throat of a writhing Dragon, and a second mouth at the end of the tail was tearing at the Dragon's face. Sadie shuddered. The creature's arms were covered by leathery wings that ended in long pinchy fingers, each with an inch-long claw. Sadie squeezed her eyes shut, but even behind the lids she could still see the terrible monsters staring back at her.

"Who would think up something like that?" she whispered.

"I think I know where we are now," Xpql replied in a hollow voice. "These must be the catacombs of the Barbazion, where they lay their dead. Rsmgt once told me about it. She told me they believe they will go to another place after death, and they leave their dead with supplies for the journey—baskets of food and jugs of water and jewels to bribe their way out of Hell. And that is where we are."

"Their bodies are *here?*" Sadie whispered.

And they were. In the red light from Xpql's eyes, they saw them in niches all around the walls: bodies tightly wrapped in cocoons of linen, like Egyptian mummies. And like Egyptian mummies, each had an elaborate headdress of what its face looked like in life. Sadie bent down to look at the mask in the dim light and then jumped back: the face was beaked, with a ring of rancorous eyes, the head bald like a skull.

"This is my Mountain Time, indeed," Xpql breathed. "We are not supposed to know what the enemy looks like until we reach our Time of Fire, and now I know why. It is too much, this knowledge."

Now that they knew where they were, they searched even harder for a way out. Sadie's nerves were stretched to the breaking point. Every step seemed to announce to the enemy that they were there in the catacombs, no matter how quietly they tried to step. Even their whispers echoed through the empty rooms, so that Sadie despaired of them ever quieting again. But the silence was worse. As they tiptoed along the tunnels, kicking small pebbles of lava out of their way, Sadie thought she heard small scuffling feet behind them. But despite her fear and caution, she let out a shriek when they came upon the Dragon bones. The cry resounded for a long time until it died out in a whisper.

"So it is true what my People say," Xpql sighed, contemplating the skeleton. "'Dreams are but fantasies, but all nightmares are true.' Rsmgt always said the Barbazion captured my People to wall them up alive when they buried their leaders."

It was too much—and these were the monsters that were holding her sister captive. "Poor Phoebe . . ." Sadie choked. She remembered the look on her sister's face that last night at home when she had asked Sadie to tell her, "Be safe," and she felt sick to her core. She sank to her knees; there was nothing to stop the tears.

Xpql stared at her in consternation. "What's wrong?" he cried, bending down and staring at her. "You're leaking!"

"I can't help it," Sadie sobbed. "It's just Phoebe . . . and my parents . . . and Picker and . . . and I'm so scared!" and she lay down on the ground and began to bawl.

Xpql raced from side to side, shaking his head. "This is not good!" he muttered, as if to himself. "This is not good at all! Grandmother! Why did you not tell me about this? You said the Sadie was very strong! You did not tell me she would start to leak! Sadie-Human," he cried, "how long do we have before you leak entirely away? What shall I do?"

It was then that they both heard it: the sound of a creaking door, and then footsteps. In a moment, misery was erased by terror. Sadie never remembered running as fast as she did through those crisscrossing caves; they turned this way and that, and found their way blocked not by stone, but by wood.

In a flash, Sadie turned away from the dead end, but she saw to her horror that a black shape was advancing towards them, holding up a torch. The light was so bright that Sadie had to turn her head, but then it was dark again, and another door was shutting on them with a clang, trapping them in a tiny alcove. With a cry, Xpql sprang forward and slammed his bulk into the door to keep it from closing, spitting out smoke so hot it singed Sadie's hair as she threw her own weight against the door. A bright crack of light appeared around the door's edge, and it seemed for a minute as if they were going to succeed. They were just pulling back for a final charge when something on the other side gave a tremendous push. In the sudden blackness, they heard the sound of an iron bolt shooting home.

Through the door they heard a murmur of voices, and the sharp sound of orders being given. Involuntarily, Sadie glanced towards the wooden door on the far side of the room. Xpql shone his light on it, and they could see that there was no handle on their side. But pressing their ears against it, they thought they heard sounds, and when a breeze blew by Sadie's face from a little crack, she began to suspect that perhaps this was the door out of the caves and back to the light. Xpql must have thought the same thing, for suddenly he threw himself against the outside door with a grunt and a great exhalation of smoke.

"What are you doing?" Sadie hissed at him. "You'll crack your skull open!" But Xpql didn't answer. He took another deep breath and a running start—the door shivered on its hinges but held. Xpql drew another breath, coughed twice, and slammed himself against the door. He was breathing heavily.

"Xpql!" Sadie cried. "Stop it! You're going to hurt yourself!"

Xpql shook his head and coughed asthmatically. "The Princess," he explained, panting heavily. "Fire and Water might not protect her—we are all she has. I will not wait here to be slaughtered, when I could be finding a way to rescue her."

Behind them, behind the door that led into the catacombs, there was the sound of more commotion. Xpql picked himself up, made ready for the next run, when he suddenly stopped, one clawed hand pressed to his chest as if in great pain.

Sadie saw it, and her heart hurt. "Oh, Xpql," she said. "What happened? Do you think you broke a rib or . . ."

An expression of great agony was passing over the Dragon's face, and Sadie ran to his side. He waved her away with a weak hand, stood, staggered, and was still. Behind them, the voices were more distinct. Then Xpql raised his head to the ceiling, and howled.

The sound of it was so bone-rattling loud, so heart-chillingly fearsome that Sadie felt her heart stop in her chest. On the other side of the door, she could hear the clatter of dropped torches and the scurrying of feet, but Xpql raised himself up to his full and terrifying height, balanced himself on his tail, opened his mouth, and coughed. But it was not a cough that came out. A magnificent jet of fire spurted out of his nose and throat and incinerated the door in front of them: the early gray light of dawn poured in. A familiar rude sound came out of Xpql's mouth then, and he covered his face delicately with one of his front feet.

"Excuse me," he said to Sadie.

"You did it," Sadie congratulated him wildly. "You got your fire, and you freed us! Now we can fly out of here!"

That was the last thing she remembered before she was hit on the head.

12

Rescue

For a moment, when she opened her eyes, Sadie thought she was back at home. There was a human face staring kindly down at her, and a human hand stroking her aching head. Then whoever it was reached for a glass of water, and Sadie saw the wings. That was how she knew she was dead.

"Are you an angel?" she asked timidly.

Whoever it was laughed, a silvery, musical sound. "I'm so glad to see you awake," the angel answered, coming back to Sadie's bedside and laying her hand against Sadie's cheek. "Oh, you poor little thing, you have been so very bruised and battered! We weren't sure you would ever wake up again." She clucked over Sadie, helping her drink the water, and gently rearranging her blankets and cushions. If Sadie closed her eyes, she might have thought she was back at home with Mrs. Fitz Edna, but she did not want to close her eyes. The person who attended her was so very beautiful she felt she never wanted to close them again.

"You *are* an angel, though, aren't you?" she pressed. "I'm dead, aren't I?"

The person laughed then and called her a funny thing.

"Haven't you been listening? We thought you *would* be dead, but the Protector of all that is Good has seen to it that you should open your eyes again. Here, drink this—you need it. If you need anything else, just ask. My name is Hanaloni."

Sadie stared after the angel as she walked away. Hanaloni wore a skirt that looked as if it were made of three or four cloths tied around her slender waist: gold, red, and pale blue. Her filmy shirt left the back bare, letting the wide blue-green wings free. The wings were not covered with feathers, but were more like the shimmering scales of a butterfly, and though they were obviously useless for flight, they were as gorgeous as the impractical tail of a peacock. But it was Hanaloni's face that was the most beautiful of all: a humanlike face, with round dark eyes set perfectly in perfect dark golden skin, framed by long waving locks of auburn hair held back loosely by a scarf of apple green.

Sadie struggled to sit up, though it felt as if someone were whacking her on the forehead with an anvil. She looked around the large room. Candles flickered around its circular walls, and the walls seemed to flicker, too, until Sadie realized she was in a tent. A hole above her bed led up to the sky, where the stars twinkled against the black. The wind rushed wildly outside, but inside she was warm and cozy. The walls of the tent and the carpets on the floor and the blankets on the bed were all of the most sumptuous materials, cloth that on Earth would be called velvet and satin and brocade; thin gossamer curtains hung from the ceiling to make little rooms. A fire crackled merrily in a little stove in the middle, and Sadie smiled to smell something cooking on its top. But something was missing.

"Where is Xpql?" she asked in concern, when Hanaloni returned.

Hanaloni wrinkled her honey-colored brow. "Xpql?" she asked, stumbling distastefully over the strange sound.

"My friend, the one who was with me in the cave. The Dragon."

"Dragon?" Hanaloni repeated. In her mouth, the word bore as much similarity to English as a toddler's scribble might resemble a Dragon picture. "We did not see any friend when we found you. You were alone in the cave, except for . . ."

"Except for what?"

"I wasn't sure if you'd remember." Hanaloni rolled back on her heels and gave Sadie a pitying look. "When we found you, little one, it was not a minute too soon. One of the Barbazion was standing over you. . . ."

Sadie imagined the beaked face coming close to her skin, and she shuddered even in the heat of the fire. Then she thought of Xpql and fell back heavily on the pillow.

"They must have captured him," she said sadly. "He was so scared of being captured. . . . Poor Xpql! Maybe he should have died on the mountain."

In a fluid motion, Hanaloni knelt down beside her, trying to smooth the sad memory from Sadie's brow.

"I am sorry about your friend," she said gravely. "We did not have time to search for anyone else—it was all we could do to drive the Barbazion away. But do not despair entirely—I do know where there is another of your kind."

"*Phoebe!*" Sadie cried, jumping up again. "Did you rescue her?"

"She is female, then?" Hanaloni asked with interest. "We were not sure. She resisted our people strongly when we attempted to give her new clothes, for hers were wet through, and the nights are cold. We found her wandering, quite alone, far to the north. She does not seem to understand anything we ask her."

"Oh, poor Phoebe!" Sadie said, half in anxiety and half in relief. She smiled a little, thinking of how stubbornly her sister would resist being dressed in filmy scarves—Phoebe despised everything girlie with a Dragon-like fierceness. "Poor, poor Phoebe! I have to get to her—"

"Lie down, little one," Hanaloni soothed. "You must rest now, but tomorrow night we will move on."

"But the Barbazion move at night—we should travel during the day!"

"Hush, hush," said Hanaloni with an indulgent smile. "We *do* have some experience with the Barbazion, after all. We know when to engage them, and when to hide. And even if the enemy moves in the dark, the dark is not our enemy. It hides us from enemy eyes and it gives relief from the desert heat—which is why we say that the Protector gave night as a gift to the People."

"But the Barbazion . . ."

Hanaloni put her smooth hand on Sadie's head. Her skin was remarkably soft, like a baby's, and the smell that came off her was the smell of jasmine. Sadie closed her eyes. She felt an odd sensation and tried to put a name to it: it was safety. She felt safer with this small and delicate creature than she had ever felt with the mighty Dragons. It was very strange.

"You should not worry," said Hanaloni firmly. "You are among the People—the Lalawani—now. Our band has been moving against the Barbazion for these past few months, and where we strike, we strike hard. The tribes to the north have developed a new weapon, and soon it will be ours, too. With it, the Lalawani have been driving the Barbazion from our desert, and soon we will drive them from the grasslands as well to reclaim our heritage. They have terrified us long enough."

She spoke so fiercely she seemed to grow taller, and her honey-gold skin flushed red.

"That's just what I told Xpql!" Sadie declared. "I told him we can't let the Barbazion go on like this! Oh, I'm so glad I found you! And I'm so glad you found Phoebe! I . . ." Suddenly her face fell and she looked up at Hanaloni with worried eyes. "Are you sure I'm not dead?" she asked at last. "It just seems like I woke up to everything I wanted—everything except home and my parents and Picker, that is. And Xpql. I *do* hope he managed to escape."

"Of course he did," said Hanaloni absently. She leaned down and brushed Sadie's brow with her lips. "Besides," she said, "soon the day will come that none of us will need to fear the Barbazion again. There are those who say that your presence and that of the other Wingless One is a sign that the Protector has blessed us, and I, for one, believe them. And now, little one, lie down and sleep. May the Protector grant you dreams that are sweet."

Sadie slept for the rest of the night, and for most of the next day as well. She had not known she could be so tired. She woke once, in midday. The dark cloth of the walls blocked most of the fierce noon light, and someone had covered the smoke hole, but all along the seams the sun forced its way in.

When she saw Sadie was awake, Hanaloni hovered over her, feeding her some savory stew and a soothing drink. There were other Lalawani there in the tent now, all equally beautiful, their faces noble and determined and very fierce. Some were clearly warriors, and wore armor made out of wood that seemed to glisten with water. Several Lalawani crouched down, polishing wooden helmets, fastening feathers to arrows or waxing what looked like long and lethal bows. Sometimes they sang, and their songs were strange and harsh and sad, like the desert. A few young Lalawani stood about, moving the hot air with broad fans.

Sadie was bursting with questions as the afternoon wore on, but Hanaloni hushed her with a hand. The light was growing dim now, and everyone was busy. Several Lalawani knelt on the floor, rolling up the thick dark wall coverings, and revealing the light-colored outer cloth that deflected the brutal rays of the sun. An older woman, hunched and wrinkled, but still moving with the noble grace of the others, was taking apart the stove, while others rolled up the rugs, revealing the hard, lava-studded ground beneath. Soon the only things left inside the tent besides Sadie were her own bed and blankets. From outside, there came a coordinating call, and then a whoosh of wind. The cloth covering pulled away from the frame, flapped for a moment in the breeze, and was pulled out of view. Sadie was left in the middle of the desert under a frame of wood.

Sadie looked around with interest. It was like a little city of tents, there, in the desert. A dozen or more stood around on the speckled plain, in various states of deconstruction, and everywhere Lalawani hurried with bags and bundles, their long wings trailing elegantly behind them. A caravan of what looked like horses stood patiently at the edge of the camp, and in the rare quiet moments, Sadie could hear them stomp and whinny. She stood up out of bed, wobbled a little, and sat down.

A tall Lalawani, bearded, entered the room with a hammer in his hand. His crimson clothing showed off the sinewy muscles of his arms and legs, and Sadie thought she had never seen such a handsome man, not even in the movies. She blushed a little when he looked at her, but she could not take her eyes off him as he took aim with his hammer at the very middle of the tent. He hit the place where the smoke hole was outlined by the interlocking poles of the ceiling, and the poles came loose just enough to let him lift them down, one by one. He took them out in a circular pattern, until only four remained holding up the frame, and then he turned to Sadie.

"I know your kind," he said gently. "You like to see a job well done. Come, let me move you, and you can tell me if I am doing my job as I should." His eyes twinkled at her then, and Sadie felt complimented and teased and pleased and embarrassed all at once. She blushed when he leaned down and picked her up in his arms, but in a moment her embarrassment was changed to amazement. He was so strong his muscles seemed to be made of iron or wood, and although Sadie was not light, he carried her out of the tent as easily if she had been Phoebe. He winked at her then, and Sadie blushed some more as other Lalawani came forward and gathered the poles into bunches. The tent was gone. The tall Lalawani shouldered his hammer jauntily, winked at Sadie once more, and strode off. He whistled as he walked, a mournful tune, but Sadie had never seen anyone so thoroughly contented in all her life.

"I see you've met Arananu," Hanaloni said at Sadie's shoulder. Together, they gazed after the man in red. "Now you have seen the best we have to offer, and our best hope against the Barbazion. But here, stand up—I have brought you clothes."

Sadie looked down at the stained and tattered flannel of her pajamas. She felt ridiculous wearing her battered nightclothes, but she knew she would feel even more outrageous arrayed in flowing scarves. "Thank you," she said, blushing. "But I think I'll keep mine."

"Take this one, at least," Hanaloni said, wrapping a warm cloak around Sadie's shoulders. "We call it the-tent-that-moves, for it protects us from wind when we move at night. Come now—I've found you a place on the wagons."

She pointed to the edge of the camp, where Sadie could see four horselike creatures harnessed to wagons: great white horses that whickered to one another. But when they grew close enough, Sadie gasped. They were not horses, after all, but unicorns—unicorns with long pearly horns and delicate, pearly hooves. Sadie stared.

"Oh!" she said to Hanaloni. "Can I *touch* one?"

It was just like when she was a child, when she had gone to the pony farm and fallen in love with a little bay Morgan named Cap'n Ichabod. She'd loved that horse with such a consuming passion that no matter how many times she visited, she'd cried each time they left the stables. But now, staring at the unicorns, Sadie knew her fierce desire for the Morgan was nothing compared to how much she wanted to own a unicorn. If anyone had been able to get her attention at that moment, and had asked her whether now that she was standing next to the unicorns she was glad that she had been brought to Dragonland, she very well might have said yes. *Yes, yes,* she would have said, *worth it, a thousand times worth it.* It was worth it, to stand beside the unicorns with their silver purity—she stepped forward, and tried to pat one next to its gray-flecked ear. The unicorn leaned over and snapped at her with its big teeth.

"Watch out, small one," Hanaloni said. "They are never quite tame. You do not want to get too close to the horns, either." Sadie looked up and saw that each horn had been topped with a ball of silver to protect against goring. She nodded, but her throat still burned with the fire of longing.

Hanaloni helped her into the wagon, which was already filled with blankets and the soft sides of the tents. Wrapping Sadie more tightly in her cloak, she covered her with more blankets.

"I never asked your name," she said at last, smiling down on the girl.

"Sadie," Sadie answered.

Hanaloni tried the name over and over in her mouth, each time making a little face as if the name tasted bad.

"May I call you Sadu?" she asked at last. "It is an old name, and means Bright-Sword. It is a noble name, and easier to say."

Sadie nodded. Once more she found that lying down reminded her of her weariness. She closed her eyes to quiet the hammering of her head.

"Then rest here, small Sadu. I will bring you food when we stop for stew time. Until then, sleep. You will need it, if you are to be our Bright-Sword against the Barbazion."

13

The Night Rider

The caravan snaked across the plain. A few Lalawani who carried torches used them to make fantastic patterns against the black of the night. Others spoke quietly among themselves, occasionally breaking into melancholy song. Sadie rode in the wagon, nervously looking up at the sky to make sure no Barbazion were flying there, their leathery wings rippling in the wind. But the sky was empty, except for a brightness in the east, and at last Sadie saw the enormous yellow moon pulling itself over the horizon. Its markings were very different from the craters that made the face on the Earth's moon: the moon in Dragonland had a dark shadow in the middle that made it look like an eye. Sadie was just about to mention this to

Hanaloni when the moon cleared the horizon entirely. At that moment, the whole caravan stopped. Every person there suddenly and silently knelt on the ground and covered his or her eyes—everyone but Sadie, that is, who stared at them, dumbfounded.

A chant came up from the kneeling figures—a low, harsh, private chant, a chant that began slowly, and then rose faster and faster until it was so hauntingly quick and loud that it made every hair on Sadie's body stand on end.

In a few minutes, the moment was past. The kneelers jumped to their feet, and each ran to his or her appointed tasks. Some assembled the little stoves from the tents; some carried huge wineskins and water jugs. Others lit great torches or whetted their knives, while still more brought out big pots or ropes of vegetables. Hanaloni passed by, carrying a rolled rug. She assured Sadie that food was coming.

"What was that about?" Sadie asked.

Hanaloni put down the heavy rug and smiled. "How funny that you do not know! The moon is full tonight, so we celebrate. The moon is the eye of the Protector, you know, and when the Protector is pleased with us, the eye grows large, and so we feast and give thanks." Her face grew more solemn as she went on. "But then, when the eye is as open as an eye can be, it looks down on the sins of the world and begins to close again in sadness. And in those times of the Closing we try—we *try*—to be better, to be more worthy, and to show our earnestness—so we neither eat nor drink when the moon shines in the sky. Little by little our efforts please the Protector, and when it seems darkest—when we feel the Protector's displeasure fullest—then the Protector has always thought kindly of us and our efforts, and the eye opens once more. And tonight the Protector has opened the eye fully once again, and we shall feast. . . ."

Her eyes were shining as she went on. "And perhaps, this time, the eye will not close. There are some who believe our holy war will change all that. Arananu says that once we rid the land of the Barbazion, the eye will never close again. I do not know if it is true, although I trust him. . . ." She gazed out over the crowd, and her eyes fell on Arananu, who was standing among a group of Lalawani, his head thrown back and laughing.

"Arananu says that the signs are multiplying that our war pleases the Protector," Hanaloni went on. "Just before the fighting with the Barbazion began, the Protector brought night to us during the day. It was an awesome sight, like a door rolling across the hot sun, shutting it out long enough for us all to see the holy darkness. And since that time, we have taken courage and moved against the Barbazion, just as the cool of night moved against the sun."

Sadie remembered the eclipse that had signaled Phoebe's birth, and thought about how the Dragons, too, had seen it as some sort of divine sign. But thinking of the Dragons only made her think of Mrs. Fitz Edna, and Xpql, wherever he was, and of poor Phoebe locked in the tower, and she started feeling anxious to continue moving towards her sister.

"And Phoebe—" she interrupted. "The other one who looks like me, I mean—is she close? When will I see her?"

Hanaloni laughed her beautiful laugh. "You *are* impatient," she chided. "I would say, 'Soon, soon, Sadu,' but I know nothing is soon to one who longs. But the time will go faster if you eat. They are catching fresh meat now, and then we will feast." She shouldered her awkward load once more and walked over to the group around Arananu. She spread out the rug beside him and waited for him to sit before she hurried over to the Lalawani who were chopping vegetables.

Sadie looked around. On the edge of all the commotion, three Lalawani stood stock-still, each with an arm held straight out, armed with leather. Then she saw an owl-like bird come winging softly over the plain, landing on one of the outstretched arms as if lighting on a branch.

"What are those birds catching?" Sadie asked when Hanaloni returned with a cup of cool water.

"Small birds, I assume, or a djinalane. They are too small to catch anything larger, which is unfortunate. But the Barbazion slaughtered the last of our hunting dogs the last time the eye was shut, so we are grateful for what small meat we get."

Sadie's stomach was growling long before Hanaloni came back, holding a small bowl. Before handing it to Sadie, she closed her eyes and murmured a prayer to the Protector. Sadie waited impatiently, clutching her spoon in her hand. When Hanaloni opened her eyes, Sadie thrust the spoon into the bowl. The stew was glistening with fat and thick with orange vegetables floating among the meat and bones. Sadie salivated, and spooned out a bite of the succulent-looking meat.

Suddenly she stopped, the spoon halfway to her mouth. The bone in the bowl was tiny, a tiny bone from a tiny bird, a little bird like the one who had befriended her in the swamp. She laid down the spoon with a sick and guilty feeling.

In the end, though, she ate it. After all, the bird was already dead, and she was really very hungry.

The unicorns were getting tired. They balked when the terrain grew rougher, and towards dawn they refused to move forward at all, no matter how much the Lalawani shouted and cracked their whips. The drivers paused, conferred, and at last the orders went up to stop for the upcoming day.

Two young Lalawani appeared by Sadie's side, and began to unhitch the unicorns. The animals stood still, and hung their heads morosely. The arrogance of the early evening was gone in their exhaustion. Sadie reached out her hand and touched one's sweat-flecked withers. The unicorn shuddered his skin but suffered her to pat him. He turned to Sadie with red-rimmed eyes, and she pulled her hand away. She did not like to see that defeated look in his noble eyes.

She turned instead to where the Lalawani were putting up the tents for the day, and once she started watching, she could not stop. It was like a beautiful dance, that tent raising. Some moved this way, holding the tent poles, and others stood still, waiting with the heavy cloth of the walls until the moment when the dancers gracefully fastened both elements together. Arananu walked among the other Lalawani, wielding his heavy hammer, and everywhere he went he was greeted with laughter. He walked by Sadie, and winked, and then continued on his way, and his shoulder muscles rippled above the fluttering black-and-orange wings.

Hanaloni was by Sadie's side. "I know you would have liked to reach your Phoebe tonight," she said, handing Sadie a bowl of water, "but the beasts were tired, and we could not have traveled much longer before the heat."

A sudden commotion interrupted her. She turned towards the sound, and over her shoulder Sadie saw a rider bending over the neck of an enormous unicorn, whipping it into a gallop out of the camp. Before it disappeared out of sight, the flash of black-and-orange wings told Sadie that the rider was Arananu.

They watched him disappear into the gray sameness of the horizon, and then Hanaloni led Sadie inside one of the noisy tents. She tucked Sadie into a soft bed beside the stove, but Sadie could not sleep. She tried to hear in the indistinct murmur of the Lalawani the comforting sounds of her parents talking with guests downstairs. She imagined for a moment she would awake up in the morning and go see Picker. *All right,* she said to her friend in her head. *Maybe you're right. I should have read more fantasy novels. They might have prepared me for this.*

Then she slept. When she woke, the tent was like a bustling hive. Sadie watched the Lalawani at their work, a little lonely in the midst of their activity, and a little hurt that no one wanted to ask her about herself, not even where she came from. But the Lalawani seemed too busy for curiosity. As on the day before, some of them worked at preparing food while others repaired their weapons. Across the room, one fierce-looking Lalawani was attaching feathers to a pile of arrows. Sadie was surprised to see how young she looked—if she had been human, she might have been no more than sixteen.

The Lalawani startled when she saw Sadie looking at her. Then, very deliberately, she grabbed a fistful of the fletched arrows and strode across the tent towards the stove. Sadie waited expectantly for her to speak, but instead the Lalawani took the top off a boiling pot and viciously stabbed her arrows into it.

Then, as if she'd made up her mind, she squared her shoulders with their red-and-gold wings and turned to Sadie. Her round eyes glittered as she spoke.

"You are Sadu, the Bright-Sword," she whispered urgently. "They say you are here to bring us luck against the Barbazion."

"I hope so," Sadie stammered.

"My name is Olani," the Lalawani went on in her quick,

hard voice. She leaned forward so that her breath tickled Sadie's ear. "I can't say this to anyone else," she whispered, "but you were sent by the Protector . . ." She looked around furtively before going on. "Tell me the truth, Sadu. Is it true what my brother Ochanu and the others say? Is it true we will all die in the coming days, unless every Barbazion lies bloody at our feet? Will we never be safe unless we pass through an ocean of blood?"

Her voice was shaking as she went on without waiting for an answer. "If you really came from the Protector, Sadu, you must have strengths and powers. Is there anything I can do to have you protect me? I can no longer sleep. I cannot bear it, not knowing each morning if my death day has come. Please, Sadu, please! I do not want to die! Bring my plea to the Protector. Let me live to see the destruction of the Barbazion so I can live one day, at least, without fear. Please, Sadu!"

Sadie did not know what to say. Olani gave her a stricken look and bowed her head. "I understand," she sighed. "Your silence is the answer to my prayer." She covered her eyes with the flat of her hand in a ritual farewell, and backed away.

The tent was bustling now. Just as the night before, the solid-looking structure was unpacked and dismantled. A different Lalawani was wielding the heavy hammer now, without the strength and confidence of Arananu, but still the tents came down with astonishing rapidity. Sadie watched them all, but the pleasure of the work was spoiled by her memory of Olani's fear.

The wagons were packed as before, and Hanaloni helped Sadie onto a wagon as before, and once more they continued over the desert. As before, Sadie was hungry long before they stopped, and she waited eagerly for the moon to come up so they could feast again. But when the moon poked above the horizon, the caravan suddenly stopped with a collective wail. Sadie looked around in consternation; the Lalawani were all looking up at the sky and keening as if their hearts would break. Sadie jumped to her feet, scanning the horizon to see the approaching Barbazion that signaled their death, but the horizon was empty, except for three jagged basalt formations, and the yellow moon that hung there, nearly full, but not quite full.

"What is it?" she asked the nearest Lalawani, but he was too busy cutting at his forehead with a piece of pumice in an act of ritual mourning to answer. Then Sadie remembered that Hanaloni had told her that the Lalawani took the waning moon as a sign of displeasure from their Protector, and she remembered unhappily that in those times they fasted to win back their Protector's trust. Her hungry stomach began a wail of its own.

Then, horribly, the ritual wail around her began to change into fear. A few Lalawani pointed to the south. Way off on the horizon, where the moon lit up the three rock formations against the sky, something was moving.

All around her, the Lalawani flew to protect the caravan. The wagons were arranged in a circle, and the protective balls were taken from the ends of the unicorns' horns. The youngest Lalawani were lifted into the wagon beside Sadie, and each lay still on the wagon's bottom, hiding head and chest in a protective ball. Someone pushed Sadie's head down, too, but as soon as they were alone, Sadie stood up and stared.

The Lalawani had sprung up to the top of the wagons, weapons ready. They stood as still and silent as rock; only their hair and their spectacular wings moved in the wind. A profound silence settled upon the scene. Sadie looked at the other children. They were very young, not older than Phoebe, but even they lay very still, as if they understood that their lives might depend upon their silence. And perhaps they did. For the first time since the Lalawani had rescued her from the Barbazion, Sadie felt the cold sick chill of fear.

Whatever it was was coming closer. Sadie could feel the mounting tension. Then, involuntarily, her hands clenched into fists. She refused to be stopped by the Barbazion when she was so close to Phoebe; she gritted her teeth and swore she would not stop fighting until Phoebe was back home. Someone gave a shout then, as if giving voice to Sadie's own anger, and the archers jumped from the wagons and rushed off towards the approaching hoofbeats. Sadie peeked up over the edge of the wagon, and saw. It was Arananu, not a hundred feet away, and he had a small wingless rider tied to the unicorn before him.

"Phoebe?" Sadie gasped, and she leapt from her hiding place. Arananu bounded from the back of the animal just as Sadie reached him, and the wingless rider in front slid a little to the side. Sadie stared.

It was too big to be Phoebe, but at the same time, the rider was decidedly human. Cautiously, Sadie crept forward. The person, whoever it was, raised its head, and Sadie saw the cowlick that twisted up to the sky. The eyes that stared out of the pale face were hollow and haunted, but Sadie thought she knew them.

"Picker?" she guessed.

14

His Story

Picker slumped against Sadie in the wagon, tired and drawn and wan. In the few days since she'd seen him last, he had aged. He still had the baby fat in his face, and the silly yellow cowlick that made him look like a character in a cartoon, but his eyes were haggard and haunted like the eyes of someone who has seen too much.

He looked tired, sick, and hungry. When the caravan stopped again, Sadie jumped from the wagon and looked for something for Picker to eat. She saw Olani and caught her roughly by the arm.

"Please," Sadie cried, "my friend—he's so weak—can't we get him some food?"

Olani stared at Sadie with a shocked expression. "But, Sadu . . . the moon . . ."

"He's starving, look at him! He needs *food!*"

Olani looked up at the misshapen eye and whispered angrily: "Are you tempting me to break my vows, to see if I am worthy of protection? I am not so weak, Sadu—I will not be tempted by compassion."

"But . . ." Sadie protested as Olani stalked off. She looked back towards the wagon. In the pale moonlight, Picker looked almost green.

"Picker," she said miserably. "Picker, I'm so sorry—I can't get you any food—the Lalawani are fasting. . . ." She looked down and thought she would happily give him her own fingers to gnaw on if it would make the horrible haunted look leave his face.

Then she remembered. "Picker! I do have something that might help you. . . . I have some Dragon blood—it's helped me heal and not be hungry and cold since I got it. I could give some to you—except it might hurt a little."

Picker looked up. His eyes were so full of pain she could not imagine any more would make a difference. Before he could object, Sadie pulled out the knife Hanaloni had given her for protection against the Barbazion, and drew it against her palm as she had seen people do in movies. She cut herself without flinching, with a fair amount of pride that she could show Picker how brave she had become since she came to

Dragonland, and how much she was willing to do for him now that he had joined her there. He hesitated for a moment after she handed him the knife, and winced as he made a quick cut. Sadie reached out and grabbed his hand, pressing her wound to his, and stared fiercely at his pale face, as if willing it to become pinker. They rode along like that for many miles over the bumpy desert, their blood mingling together.

Towards dawn, the moment had not yet seemed right to ask him how he had traveled all that way to Dragonland, and what had happened to him since she left him tinkering with the robot in his garage. For many miles now, all she had managed to say to her friend was "it's okay, it's okay, it's okay," which, even if it might be a lie, seemed the best she could do. Then, as the darkness started breaking in the east, the caravan stopped and began to set up camp. Hanaloni reappeared with her sympathetic eyes and a calabash of cold water. When they had drunk, she led them away from the others to a small tent that had been pitched in the middle of the compound.

"The Protector gives us many good things," she said, "and one of them is privacy. This small hut is where unmarried couples meet to decide to marry, and where married couples come to decide to unmarry. Here is where babies come to be born in peace, and where the dying come to leave in peace. And now, as we have no one marrying and birthing in this time of war, and no one yet dying, thanks be to the Protector, the hut is empty. I offer it to you." She held open the door and waited for Sadie and Picker to crawl inside.

"I understood her," Picker said thickly. His voice creaked a little, like a door long unopened. "Why could I understand her? I never could, with the others. Is she speaking English? It doesn't sound like English, but I understood every word."

"It's the Dragon blood I gave you," Sadie explained. "I can even understand animals with it. But Picker, Picker . . . what happened? How did you get here?"

Picker sighed, and turned his wounded eyes to her before looking back at the floor.

"I followed you," he said at last. "I came to rescue you."

Now it was Sadie's turn to be embarrassed—or rather, seventy percent embarrassed and thirty percent pleased. "Thank you," she said, looking away.

"There wasn't anything else I could do," Picker told the floor. "I thought you were counting on me."

"Thank you," Sadie said again. "But why . . . ?"

Picker's voice was very miserable, "I had to," he explained. "Your parents showed me the note you left: *Tell Picker I'm sorry I won't be there to help with the robot.* They thought *I* would know what it meant."

"What do you mean? Couldn't they read it?"

"Of course they could *read* it, they just couldn't *understand* it. And I couldn't either. They were just standing there with the police, staring at me, and everyone was so serious, so worried, and I had no idea at all what it meant."

"I told them not to worry!" Sadie snapped with indignation. "That's why I wrote the note in the first place!"

"What did you think, Sadie?" Picker interrupted. "How could they *not* worry? No one knew where you were! Everyone thought that Phoebe was kidnapped, and that you'd gone after her to save her, and that you'd written the note in code—and they thought because *my* name was on the note, I would know what it meant. . . ."

He moved a little on his seat and turned his face towards the wall.

"But I didn't know what it meant," he muttered. "I thought you were being kept somewhere and that the note was meant to tell me where and that you were counting on me to know what you meant."

His voice trailed off before he started again.

"So I thought about that last day, when we were swimming in the quarry, and how I had joked that the secret tunnel might really be there under the water. Remember how we said we should send the robot to look into the tunnel? So I thought you were there. I know it was dumb. It was just that there was this stupid fantasy part of me that thought I could find you magically alive in some stupid magic cave, even though everyone else knew you were dead."

He was blushing now, and he slapped angrily at his cowlick.

"So I took that stupid underwater flashlight we bought that time, and went to the quarry at like five o'clock in the morning. No one was there—it was all misty and creepy, but I jumped right in. It was *freezing,* Sadie. It was so cold I didn't think I was going to be able to swim. I flailed around there trying to keep my mouth above the surface and thought, *This is it, I'm going to die.* I could see the headlines—IDIOTIC BOY, 11, DROWNS IN IDIOTIC ATTEMPT TO LOCATE FRIEND'S BODY. WHAT A DOPE. And that was when I knew that heroic gestures are for jerks."

"You're not a jerk," contradicted Sadie. "And Picker, even if I wasn't there, it was really br—"

"I didn't say it wasn't *brave,*" Picker said, finishing her sentence just like he always did. "I just said it was *stupid.* I really could have drowned there, you know. I'm not that good a swimmer, and it was *really* cold."

"But what happened?" Sadie pressed. "How did you get *here?*"

"I went to the place where we were swimming that last day," he said, his voice flat like a blank sheet of paper. "I took a deep breath, and I turned on the flashlight. And I let myself sink. The flashlight was shining on the wall, and I could totally see everything—the dynamite marks where they blasted and everything, and then I saw it, Sadie. I saw—"

"The cave?"

"Yeah. But I was out of breath, so I had to go back up. But

I went back down, faster, and I looked in. And then the light went out."

"What do you mean?"

"The flashlight. What a piece of crap! The first time I used it, and it broke. But Sadie, the weird thing, the really weird thing, was that it wasn't dark. You won't believe me, but there was another light, a blue light, a light *in* the cave." He paused. "But of course you'll believe me—you saw it, too."

Sadie shook her head. "I never saw the cave," she said.

"What do you mean?" Picker asked, astonished. "You didn't come here that way?"

"No," Sadie said. "But don't worry about me not believing you. I've seen pretty strange things myself this past week. Tell me the rest."

Picker took a deep breath. "So I'm under the water, right, looking at this light, and I put out my hand, but the water doesn't feel like water. I dunno—it was thicker or something, and I had to really push to get through it. But, Sadie—there wasn't any water on the other side of the water."

"What do you mean?"

"I mean there was like this *barrier* thing between the water and the cave, and when I pushed through it, I could breathe and everything. And all the water was next to me, not coming into the cave. And I looked towards the light, and I thought that maybe you would be there, and I started crawling towards the back, but then—I got scared. I wanted to know I could get back into the quarry, so I pushed my finger through the barrier. . . ."

"And what happened?"

"Oh, man—" he said, and it was like a little of the old Picker shining through. "I poked it, and all of a sudden all that water was pouring into the cave. It pushed me right up out of this hole, and I didn't know where on Earth I was."

"But you weren't on Earth, right?" Sadie interrupted. "You were here, right?"

"We're not on Earth?" Picker asked, looking at her for the first time.

Sadie shook her head, slowly, and she told him a bit of Phoebe's history, and some of her own, how she had flown up through the atmosphere with Mrs. Fitz Edna and entered Dragonland through some sort of portal in the air.

"Phoebe's a *Dragon?*" Picker repeated, when Sadie finished her story.

"She's still my sister," said Sadie defensively.

Picker didn't miss a beat. "I know *that,*" he said. "But she's a *Dragon* and she's *here,* on this planet?"

"Yeah," Sadie answered. Ever since Hanaloni had told her they had found another human, she had been thinking of her sister as safe, but now she was back to the miserable certainty that Phoebe was still being held captive by the Barbazion. "Yeah," she repeated, "but Picker, she's been captured by the most horrible . . . you wouldn't believe . . ."

"Yes, I would," Picker answered quickly. "I'd believe any-thing now."

". . . horrible creatures, these *monsters*. They're called the Barbazion, and these people, the Lalawani, they're fighting them, and Phoebe's Dragons are fighting them, and we can fight them too, Picker, you and I—we can fight them to-gether, and save Phoebe, and save them all!"

"No," said Picker firmly. "I won't fight, Sadie."

"What do you mean?" Sadie protested, speaking quicker in an effort to explain it to him. "You don't understand—you don't understand what these Barbazion are like—"

"Yes, I do!" Picker broke in, and in his voice Sadie heard an anguish she had never heard before. "I *saw* it, Sadie. I saw it with my own eyes, after I came out of the cave."

"What?" Sadie asked, momentarily cowed. "What was it you saw?"

Picker's voice snagged in his throat as he answered her. He was still staring at the floor. "I was standing at the edge of a wood when I came out of the cave," he said, choking. "There was no one there. I had to walk for a long time, trying to find someone, *anyone*, and finally I got to some tents . . ."

"What?" Sadie asked, as he trailed off. "What did you see?"

"Nobody." He stopped, and for the first time that she could remember, Sadie didn't even try to finish his sentence for him. She waited quietly for him to start again. At last he did. "That's what I saw. There was nobody there." He stopped again, and Sadie could taste the bitterness in his tone. "There was nobody there at all, just bodies. . . ."

"They were dead?" Sadie guessed. "Who? The Lalawani? What—"

"They weren't just *dead*, Sadie," Picker said, almost angrily. "They had been . . ." His face was very pale. Sadie reached out to touch him, but Picker pulled away.

"What?" she asked.

"I won't tell you," Picker said, shaking his head as if to scatter the memory. "I won't ever tell anyone, ever—I wouldn't want anyone else to have to remember what I remember."

Sadie said nothing.

"I kept on walking," Picker continued, in his dead voice. "I came to more tents, and it was the same thing. The people there—the Lalawani . . ." He paused miserably. "I was so tired—so scared, and hungry. . . . I took their food, Sadie. I didn't want to do it, but I was so hungry, and they weren't going to use it anymore—"

"You shouldn't feel bad about it, Picker," Sadie interrupted. "It wasn't stealing. They were d—"

Picker cut her off. "You don't understand. They were worse than dead! Whoever did that to them didn't need to make them suffer like that!"

"It must have been the Barbazion!" Sadie exploded. "That's just what the Barbazion *do!* That's why we have to fight them! The Dragons know it, the Lalawani know it, and . . . well, *I* know it!" And she told Picker everything that had happened to her since Mrs. Fitz Edna had flown down to see the destruction of Xthltg, and everything she had heard about the Barbazion from Xpql and Hanaloni. "And that's why we have to fight them," she concluded. "We *can't* let them go on like that."

To her astonishment, Picker shook his head. "I won't fight them," he declared again.

"But you don't have to be scared," Sadie assured him quickly. "Hanaloni says the Lalawani have a new weapon—"

"It's not that I'm *scared*, Sadie!" Picker interrupted. "Don't you see? I just don't want to be like anyone who *could* do that. I've seen killing now, and I *never* want to kill."

Sadie stared at him in disbelief.

"But we can't let them get away with it, Picker!" she insisted. "If we don't do anything, they'll just keep on doing what they did to the Dragons and the Lalawani . . . it's like with Hitler. You would have fought against Hitler, wouldn't you?"

"I wouldn't have needed to fight against Hitler if none of the Nazis had been willing to fight *for* Hitler," Picker answered, illogically, and Sadie threw her hands up in the air.

"Sure," she said, "but what do you do when there *are* Nazis? What then, Picker? 'Cause that's what's happening here!"

"What are *you* going to do?" he asked her. "Kill them all?"

"Well . . . yes!"

"Look," Picker said. The cowlick drooped a little as he bent his head to avoid her glare. "It can't . . . it *can't* be the answer. When I saw those Lalawani dead—well, I didn't have to know that they were the good guys. They might have been the bad guys, and I would've still been sick to my stomach that they were dead. They were *people* with families and lives, and now they're *dead*. Dead! That's the thing of it, Sadie—killing isn't the bad side effect of war. It is the *point* of war, and there's no getting around that."

Sadie stared at him. With a jolt she felt he was not the same Picker who had been her best friend for so long. Now that he was with her, she missed him more than ever.

"But you *have* to help us," she insisted. "You can't let the Barbazion keep Phoebe . . . she's just a little kid!"

Picker winced. "Don't hate me, Sadie," he said. "You didn't see what I saw."

Sadie was just opening her mouth to object when a deafening boom from outside sent them both scurrying through the entrance of the tent.

15

The Rock-Breaker

Outside, the fading echo of the explosion was replaced with triumphant cheers.

"What is it?" Sadie asked the nearest Lalawani.

"They were testing our weapon," he replied. "If it works, we move against the Barbazion tonight." A second deafening boom, and a wild cheer went up from the crowd.

Hanaloni saw them and came over. Her eyes were shining. "This is our first Rock-Breaker," she explained proudly, pointing at the horizon. Sadie barely heard. She was staring out over the plain in astonishment. Of the three volcanic upthrusts she had seen on the horizon the night before, only two remained. Boulders were strewn all over the plain, but the third rock shape was gone.

"Dynamite," Picker whispered, staring at the ceramic ovals with their protruding fuses that lay beside them.

"Do you have Rock-Breakers where you come from?" Hanaloni asked him curiously.

"Yes," Picker said in such a sour voice Sadie wanted to kick him. "A man named Alfred Nobel invented them and he founded a peace prize to make up for it."

"We did not invent the Rock-Breaker," Hanaloni explained to them. "Other Lalawani in other bands have already used it against the Barbazion. But this is the first time we have successfully created our own. Arananu was right when he said that you wingless children would bring us luck—it does look indeed as if the Protector has sent you to us."

"But how can we use the Rock-Breaker?" asked Sadie eagerly.

Hanaloni laughed. "Ah, Sadu-Bright-Sword, *we* will use it against a Barbazion city not far from here, but *you* will stay here with the other children. We are civilized, not like the Barbazion. We do not send our children into war."

"But I want to go!" Sadie protested. "It's not my fault I'm still a child—and it's not *fair* to make me stay behind, not when I can finally *do* something!"

"And what would you do, Sadu?" asked Hanaloni gently. "No, your job is to stay here, bringing us good luck."

"But it's *my* sister who's being held by the Barbazion! We *need* to rescue her—she's just a little kid!"

"There's *another* Wingless One?" Hanaloni mused. "The

good omens are multiplying. . . . Come. We must speak to Arananu."

They found Arananu far away from the edge of the camp, inspecting the damage done by the dynamite.

"Should you be so far from the others?" Hanaloni asked him with concern. "If the Barbazion came . . ."

"Let them come!" Arananu challenged. "Let them come and see what we have planned for them!" He stood there, gazing fiercely into the sky as if daring the enemy to arrive, and then his stern face relaxed, his large brown eyes crinkling and looking very friendly. "Well, my little ones," he said jovially, "are you recovered from your traumas?"

He looked at Picker affectionately and then turned to Sadie. "I was with the Olkawanu Tribe, learning about this Rock-Breaker, when we first saw this one crouching at the side of the road. He was unable to speak, more like a wingless frog than a person. The others wanted to kill him, but I said, 'No, keep him for good luck.' And so we did. And since that time, we have had nothing but good luck, haven't we, little frog? And when we found *you*, Sadu, it felt as if the Protector has been smiling down on us indeed. And this demonstration has been the proof of my faith." He waved his hand towards the empty space where the rock tower had once stood.

"I don't know if I'm bringing any sort of luck," Picker ventured, "but thanks for keeping me alive."

"So the frog has a tongue!" said Arananu, feigning surprise.

"This is a great day indeed. Will you ride with me tonight, my friends, when we destroy the Barbazion city?"

"Arananu!" Hanaloni exclaimed. "They're just children! They should stay behind. . . ."

Arananu held up his hand. "They may be children, but they have been sent to us by the Protector for luck. Wouldn't it be the height of ingratitude to leave them behind? How would you feel if the children stayed behind and all our plans failed?"

And Hanaloni had no argument to make to that.

Despite Arananu's assurances that they would not be part of the battle, Sadie spent that morning practicing with bow and arrows. It was decidedly fun. First she planted her feet, and nocked the obsidian-tipped arrow onto the bowstring. Holding her left arm very straight (to keep the bowstring from snapping against it when she let the arrow fly), she slowly pulled back with her right hand. Then with a *zing* (and a yelp when the bowstring did snap her), she let the arrow go. It flew wildly, and Arananu, lying stretched out on a blanket behind her, laughed and reminded her again to keep her body still.

"Come on, Picker!" Sadie called. "Try this—it's totally fun!"

Picker shook his head. "I already told you," he said. "I don't want any part of your war."

Sadie rolled her eyes. "Just pretend you're at camp, can't you? Remember camp? Good, clean, wholesome fun? Please, Picker? For me?"

He looked at her unhappily and rose to his feet. Arananu handed him another bow and tried to mold Picker's body into the proper form. Picker slouched sourly and did not hold the stance. On his first shot, he snapped his arm with the bowstring, but since he had pulled it back so with such little energy, it barely hurt him. Sadie, laughing at him and not paying attention, snapped her own arm and swore, and then finally Picker smiled.

"What are you laughing at?" she said, pouting. "It's not like you can do better!"

"Oh, yeah?" he challenged.

"Oh, yeah!" she answered defiantly. This was their old war cry, the war cry of their friendship—the way they had always egged each other on to throw chestnuts farther, to climb higher, to race faster.

Picker picked up the bow again. He whacked himself painfully on the arm with the bowstring, but still he kept his form, and the singing arrow sailed in a beautiful arc towards (but not quite to) the target.

"So there," he said triumphantly, throwing down the bow.

"So there?"

"So there!" This was the second sally of the war cry, the leather gauntlet thrown down at a medieval tourney. It was impossible to ignore.

"All right, then," Sadie said, tossing back her hair and accepting the challenge. She picked up her bow, cocked her head, nocked the arrow, and let loose the string. But in her haste to turn and stick her tongue out at Picker, she forgot to follow through, and the arrow flew in a feeble arc and landed short of the target. Picker laughed, and Sadie sulked, and then Picker shot an arrow that actually hit the target, and Sadie (following through this time) shot one that actually hit near the target's center, and before long Arananu declared he would need to move the targets farther away. He stood with them as the hot sun crawled up the sky, patiently correcting their form, and offering encouragement and advice.

It was getting too hot to stand out in the sun. The glare was terrific. At last Picker asked Arananu for a demonstration, and they watched in amazement as he shot seventeen arrows one after another into the center of the target or the center of arrows already shot. Sadie ran up to the target when he was done, and tried to pull the arrows from the bag of hay. Some were buried up to their feathers, and many others had been split.

"We should stop now," said Arananu, looking at the broken shafts. "Today is not the day to waste arrows. I would be happier to see each of these buried in Barbazion flesh."

Picker turned pale then and stalked back to the tents. Sadie stared after him.

"I don't know what's with him," she said, but Arananu shrugged gracefully and laid his big hand on Sadie's shoulder.

"He is not a soldier," he answered. "But you, Bright-Sword, we will make a soldier out of you yet."

Arananu's words rang pleasantly in Sadie's ears as she

strode back to the tent. She found Picker angrily peeling vegetables with the younger Lalawani. She sat next to him and helped in silence. It seemed as if there was nothing to say anymore—it seemed ridiculous to talk about the quarry or the robot or the stories of Mr. George Orwell when they both knew the Lalawani would be marching against the Barbazion as soon as the sun went down.

16

The Battle

The caravan was a smaller group now, for the very old and very young had stayed behind. Watching the little camp shrink away into nothing in the middle of that barren plain, Sadie had to admit she was glad they were going on, even if it was towards danger. Anything seemed better than sitting and waiting like a bull's-eye in the middle of a target.

Far off to the north, a series of low hills broke the monotony of the horizon. The caravan crawled slowly towards it, reaching the hills just as the moon went down. Strangely, the weary unicorns seemed eager to attack the foothills, pulling against their bits and struggling to pull the heavy loads along. When they reached the crest, Sadie understood. Up there, the desert had finally given way to great meadows, covered with whitish grass and silver flowers that sparkled in the moonlight. The unicorns stopped then; they could not be compelled to go on. Sadie could not blame them. She jumped from the wagon and felt the cool grass between her fingers, looked up at Hanaloni, and smiled.

"Starflowers," said Hanaloni, picking one for Sadie. "They only open at nighttime. In a few moments, they will be closed."

Sadie sniffed deeply. The faint smell of the starflowers was like nothing she had ever smelled: it was sort of like the jasmine smell of the Lalawani, and sort of like ginger. It was an evocative smell, one that for Sadie woke sudden memories of Phoebe she did not know she'd had: memories of Phoebe at the breakfast table, telling stories of her Dragonland, of the grandfather unicorn, the taste of starflower nectar. Sadie was swept with sadness. *This* was where Phoebe should be, here, in this meadow, not locked away in the darkness of the Glass Castle! One of the unicorns gave an unhappy whinny then, matching Sadie's mood. She turned towards it in sympathy. They were just like Phoebe. They longed for their freedom, to throw off their harnesses and roll in the meadow to get the feeling of captivity off their skin. She saw them trying to chew great mouthfuls of the moongrass despite the bits in their mouths, and with a flash she felt it was wrong for the Lalawani to keep them as beasts of burden.

Well, the Lalawani need *something to help them move around the desert,* she said to herself uncomfortably. *At least they're not like the Barbazion, who enslave the Dragons!*

Far too soon for the unhappy unicorns, the caravan set off again. They left the cool meadows and marched along the drier prairies of bluish grasses.

"Why don't the Lalawani live here?" she asked Hanaloni. "It seems it would be easier to live here than in the desert."

A spasm of fierceness passed over Hanaloni's face. "In the beginning, my People did live here," she said. "We spread across the planet, in forest, in fens, even by the shores of the sea where the great kronos swims; but little by little, the Barbazion drove us back from the fertile lands. Many times, my People have tried to return to our ancestral home, but their settlements have always been destroyed. When the Barbazion are gone—watch out, Sadu, do not step on those flowers. They release a terrible smell."

Sadie looked down and saw a fleshy pink flower growing among the sharp grasses of the prairie. She stepped over it, but towards dawn, one of the unicorns was not so attentive. There was a disgusting *pop* and a revolting stench, and after that, she and Picker were both careful to watch their feet.

As the brown sky began to brighten in the east, Sadie found that the emotion fluttering in her chest was eagerness.

"I wish Xpql were here," she said to Picker. "He didn't

think anyone could fight against the Barbazion, and here we are, doing it!"

"I'm not going to say I'm excited, if that's what you want," he answered her, his face as sour as a pickle.

"I don't understand why you came with us, if that's your attitude," she sniffed.

"To look after you, that's why—and . . ."

"And what?"

"To find some way out of this—without fighting."

"Good luck," Sadie said sarcastically. "Let's face it, Picker. There are times you have to fight."

"And *you* face it, Sadie," he said, flushing, "there are times it's better not to. Besides, don't you think you're forgetting what you're *really* supposed to do here? What about rescuing Phoebe, huh? Isn't that what we *really* should be doing?"

"What do you think I'm doing, Picker?" she practically yelled at him. "Of course I'm trying to rescue Phoebe!"

"Oh, yeah?" he challenged. "Well, tell me, how does coming to watch the Lalawani slaughter the Barbazion help Phoebe? Or are you so obsessed with revenge that you're forgetting about what's really important?"

She stopped then. It was hard to explain what happened, whether it was a vision or a premonition or just a guilty memory dislodged by Picker's words, but she suddenly heard Phoebe's small fierce voice whispering in her ear, "You didn't say 'Be safe.'"

Picker saw the change in her, and he laid his hand on her arm.

"Hey—don't worry about Phoebe, Sades," he soothed her. "She does all right. Remember when the handle fell off the bathroom door when she was inside? She did okay then, remember?"

"She cut off a big hunk of her hair with nail scissors." Sadie sniffed.

"And painted her toenails and most of her toes—"

"—with my mother's nail polish. You can still see the place on the bathtub where she did it."

"And then, remember? When your mom was almost done reattaching the doorknob and asked Phoebe what she was doing, and she said she'd just—"

"—gotten the window open and was going to jump out." Sadie laughed a little and wiped her nose.

"That's what I mean," he said. "She's very resourceful, that Phoebe. You know she is."

Picker punched her lightly on the shoulder. "But *man*, wouldn't you hate to be her jailer? Even the Barbazion couldn't be a match for her, you know? Remember when she bit me that time?" He paused. "So she's really a Dragon, huh?"

Sadie sniffed again. "I guess so."

"Explains a lot, doesn't it?"

Sadie made a little attempt at a smile.

"What do you think your parents are going to think, when she starts giving off smoke?"

Sadie laughed then, and wiped her nose on her pajama sleeve. "Thanks, Picker," she said. The sky was brightening, and she could see that the thicket of bushes to her left seemed to move on their own, their thin branches waving like an anemone's tentacles reaching out for its prey. As Sadie watched, a bird flew too close and was snared. She winced.

"We call that one the Rooted Dog," said Hanaloni at Sadie's shoulders. "Give it wide berth. But look—I came to tell you we are close to our destination."

Sadie squinted. Her tired eyes could just make out two tall spires against the misty dimness of the horizon, growing more distinct as the dawn approached.

She found that her desire for revenge swelled in her chest as the city became more real to her. The spires of the towers looked as lovely as filigree work against the sky, but if Sadie could have flattened them by herself, she would have.

"I wish we could get there faster," she said fiercely. "I can't *wait* to make them pay for everything they've done!"

Picker looked away then, but Hanaloni's kind eyes looked very serious. "You can't be more eager than I am, Sadu," she said. "My people built this city, centuries ago, before the Barbazion drove us to the desert. But I will remind you, Sadu, that you are not to take part in the battle. Arananu promised me he will send you to the protection of the woods before the battle starts." She smiled affectionately at the children. "I have become very fond of you, Sadu. I do not want to see you incinerated by Barbazion fire." She pressed Sadie's hand before hurrying off again.

Sadie had no answer to that, but she snuck a look towards Picker, who had fallen behind. Thinking of how the Barbazion had changed him, too, she felt the full force of her hatred boiling within her again.

At last, Arananu stopped the caravan at the edge of a great forest. The Barbazion city was hidden from view, behind a ridge. The Lalawani gathered around him, their weapons in their hands. Sadie glanced nervously up at the sky to see if the enemy was there, but there was only the morning star shining cheerfully in the yellow sky, as if the world it looked down upon was just as peaceful as ever.

"Here we are," said Arananu gravely to the crowd of Lalawani who stood before him. "May the Protector let us see another night together. The Olkawanu Tribe is moving towards the city on the east, and the Rashabali to the west. We have timed the attack for the moment the sun breaks over the horizon. I do not know how many Barbazion we will kill in the first attack, nor how many may remain to fight. If things go badly, come back to the forest. We can move faster than the Barbazion on foot, and they will not be able to fly through the trees." He paused and looked over his grim-faced warriors. "This is the point of no return—either we drive them from their city or they will drive the spirits from our bodies."

The Lalawani nodded to that, and began to unload their weapons from the wagons. Hanaloni appeared before Sadie with a quiver of arrows on her back, a bow slung across the front of her bulky armor.

"But you should not still be here!" she cried when she saw Sadie and Picker. "You should already be in the forest!"

Someone laughed behind them. It was Arananu. "My good-luck charms, hiding under the leaves?" he chided Hanaloni. "They were sent to us from the Protector! Do you think the Protector wants them hidden away, like things too precious to be used?"

Hanaloni looked at him fiercely. "They're *children*, Arananu. They have no place in battle."

"And I would not bring them into battle," Arananu declared. "But still, they should be where they can see the victory they will help bring about. Come, my children, you will ride with me."

To the sound of Hanaloni's feeble protests, he lifted Sadie atop one of the largest of the unicorns. Sadie sighed to feel the warm animal beneath her. The white fur under her fingers was deep and thick, more like a rabbit's than a horse's hide, and the smell that came off it was deep and earthy. Picker sat on a smaller unicorn beside her, as moved by the experience as a sack of potatoes might be, but Sadie would not let his mood spoil her own. She felt she could barely wait until the battle began.

All around her, the Lalawani were strapping on their armor, covering it with some greasy substance before putting their helmets over their heads—wooden helmets with little slits for the eyes. Most were decorated with ugly faces, hooked beaks, and black-rimmed, red eyes, and they gave Sadie a little jolt of fear when she remembered the terrible faces of the Barbazion in the catacombs. But then again, it made sense for the Lalawani to hide their beauty and make themselves look as terrifying as the enemy they moved against, and when she forced herself to look at the masks, Sadie saw in them not only horror but a kind of fierce bravery and determination.

Here and there, some of the masked Lalawani stood close to one another and bowed, as if in blessing, and then they would cover their eyes with the flat of their hands and incline their heads before turning to face the Barbazion city. The sky was growing rosy, and in its light, Sadie could see a tall wall surrounding the towering spires. There were no gates to the city, as if the enemy flew in and out and never walked upon the ground, and once more Sadie looked nervously overhead to ensure that the leather-winged, bird-headed Barbazion were not streaking towards them in the sky. But the skies were empty. There was no movement inside the city at all.

"I hope they're in there," Sadie whispered to Picker.

He said nothing.

Hanaloni came up behind them then, a beaked helmet in her hand. "Arananu says the moment of attack is at hand," she said, staring towards the city. Sadie followed her glance and saw Arananu passing through the troops, his own armor unfastened, whispering to this one and that, and here and there slapping a back with great heartiness and joviality. Everywhere he went, he laughed out loud, as if laughing at danger. Then Hanaloni took one of Sadie's hands and one of Picker's in her own.

"We will leave the ridge in a moment," she said, "but I have made Arananu promise you should stay here only until the Rock-Breakers do their work. Now *you* must promise me that you will ride back to the forest right after. Do you promise, Sadu?"

Sadie nodded, but she was distracted by Arananu, who suddenly appeared beside her, fully armored, his terrifying helmet in his hand.

"There you are!" he cried. "Now we will see the good luck the Protector has sent us through you!"

He turned to Hanaloni, and his russet eyes crinkled as he looked down on her. "It is time now, Hanaloni. I can scarcely believe this moment has finally come."

Hanaloni looked back at the children, her eyes worried. "We must go now, children," she said. "All I can do now is ask the Protector to watch over you, and trust that you will keep your promise to ride to the forest as soon as the dust has settled from the Rock-Breakers."

Arananu laughed. "Have faith, Hanaloni!" he said. "Soon you will see that the Protector has sent *them* to watch over *us*." He settled his helmet on his head, and Hanaloni covered her lovely head with a hideous leering face. Then Arananu bowed, first to Hanaloni and then to Sadie and Picker, and the two Lalawani covered their eyes with the flat of their hands as they backed away from the children. Arananu's hand fell away as he turned, but Hanaloni kept her eyes covered until she had fully turned away, as if she could not bear to see the children for the last time. Then Arananu looked over the other Lalawani, raised his hand, and gave the signal for the attack.

It was like a silent explosion. The Lalawani began running down the hill, running like water flowing out of an opened dam. They moved so quietly that Sadie could hear the unhappy snorts of the unicorns as they strained against their harnesses. Here and there she saw a few Lalawani struggling under the heavy Rock-Breakers, and her heart quickened in her chest.

"I wish Xpql were here," she said again.

Picker said nothing. He was looking towards the Barbazion city, his pale face stony and ashen at the same time. Down by the city, the Lalawani moved into position.

"What's taking so long?" Sadie complained. "The sun's almost up!"

But even as she spoke something was happening down below. Just as the sun broke over the brown edge of the world, a bright light outlined the silent city. Then there was a deafening boom. The tall towers with their graceful spires shivered, and then shook; then, with no ceremony at all, they shuddered to the ground. A cloud of dust flew up, and settled, and the towers were gone.

A great cry of triumph went up from the crowd near the city, with Sadie shouting the loudest of all. She clapped her hands and called and shouted, and she turned towards Picker to share her exaltation with him. But Picker was sitting slumped on his unicorn, looking over to where the towers had stood. Sadie thought he might be crying.

"What's wrong?" she asked him, pointing to the smoking ruins. "Didn't you see it? We're striking back at the Barbazion, destroying their city like they destroyed Xthltg—"

"I know," he agreed. "Just like they did."

He *was* crying. After years of finishing his sentences for him, Sadie knew why, and she found herself growing hot.

"What, are you saying we're just like them? 'Cause we're not—it's just that the Dragons and the Lalawani, they deserve justice for what the Barbazion have done to them! That's all I want, *justice*. What's wrong with that?" She pointed an angry finger down to where the smoke hung over the Barbazion city, and was surprised to see how much her hand was shaking.

"Because!" Picker shouted, angrily wiping at his eyes. "Because justice and revenge are not the same thing!"

Sadie stared at him, her hands on her hips. She was so busy hating Picker at that moment, with all his smug suffering, that she had to check her rising desire to smack him.

"What do you think we should do, Picker? Should we just let them continue to kill us? Is that what you want to do?"

"Look," Picker burst out with the frustrated exasperation of someone who knows he is right and can't prove it, "just because I don't know the answer doesn't mean that there isn't an answer out there! Was it wrong to question that the world was flat before people came up with the idea that it was round?"

"What the hell are you talking about?" Sadie shouted at him. "What the hell's wrong with you, anyway? When did you become this . . . this self-righteous, this . . . this person I don't know if I like anymore?" A bitter taste was in her mouth. "Don't you see what's *happening* down there?" she shrieked, pointing down to the city.

"Yes," Picker answered. "Do you?"

Sadie grunted in frustration, and wheeled her unicorn around to face the city more fully. Down below, the battle was starting in earnest. Through the dusty air and the smoke of smoldering fires, they could see black figures circling in the blackened air above the city, and the flash of arrows, and here and there, a figure that ran and fell and then ran no more.

"They're dying," she said in horror.

"Yeah," answered Picker. "They're dying. What did you think?"

Sadie began to moan. "We have to get out of here!" she said, touching her heels to the unicorn's sides as she had been taught to do with Cap'n Ichabod. The unicorn reared up slightly, and she almost slid off its wide back. She turned around to see if Picker was smirking at her, but saw he had not moved at all.

"Picker," she called out again, "we should *go!*"

"Why?"

"Why?" she repeated. "*Why?* What do you mean, *why?* Because it's dangerous, that's why!" The thought crossed her mind then that perhaps Picker had been hit on the head during his wanderings in Dragonland: it might begin to explain his unpredictable behavior. She spoke to him as if he were slightly retarded.

"There's a war going on there," she explained patiently. "I really think we're better off in the forest."

"I know there's a war going on," he said with maddening calm. "I just feel like I should share their suffering. It seems like the least I can do. It's just the way I feel, Sadie."

Sadie almost screamed in her frustration, but the sound of it was cut off by the distant cries from the city. Her heart turned cold; her hands were cold as they gripped the reins. "That must be them," Sadie said. "That must be the Barbazion." Then she stared. "No, look—" she cried out wildly. "Look! It's the Dragons! They've come! They've come!"

It was true. Through the chaos and confusion of the battle, Sadie could see six writhing shapes speeding in the air to join the fray, twisting and turning in the air like eels. From their mouths came jets of fire.

"It will be over soon," Sadie cried out with relief. "It has to, now that the Dragons are here!"

But the battle wasn't over. First one, and then another of the Dragons stiffened in the air and fell as if brought down by an arrow, and Sadie cried out. The battle was spreading like fire, and fire was everywhere in the city. Even the wooden armor of the Lalawani burned, despite their precautions, and here and there Sadie saw one tearing at the flaming wood, trying to get it off. Sadie turned her face and would not look, and prayed that it was not Hanaloni or Arananu. But even with her eyes covered, she could not block out the battle. She could not block out the cries of the wounded, nor the sickening thud of weapons on flesh. The stench of blood was in the air, and the battle did not stop. The killing went on and on, and there was nothing Sadie could do about it. She looked longingly towards the forest, and more than once had to stop herself from galloping towards it, leaving Picker behind.

"Why isn't it over?" she moaned. "Now that the Dragons are here, it should be over!" She was scared, too—as scared as she had been when the Krnsrs had come so close to grabbing her from the rock. Panic clutched her throat, and it was all she could do to wait for Picker before she raced into the forest. "Please, Picker, *please*—I don't want to see any more, please!"

"They'll still be fighting, even if we leave," Picker said evenly. "If the war is really right, we should stay and suffer with them."

"You *have* gone crazy," Sadie wailed. "Please, Picker! Let's go *now!*"

But Picker would not move. They were still up on the ridge, the unicorns whinnying from the smell of blood, when an armored Lalawani came up the slope towards them. He pulled his helmet off as he ran.

"What are you doing still here?" he shouted as loudly as he could, being winded. "You must go *now*—it is imperative. I was sent by Hanaloni. . . ."

"Hanaloni?" Sadie repeated wildly. "Is she all right?"

A look of pain passed over the face of the Lalawani, and he spoke quickly. "She asked me to do this—she asked me to make sure you are safe. Look there, the Barbazion are coming in ever greater numbers . . . you must go!"

Then his eyes widened in horror, and Sadie turned around to see what made him stop so completely. There she saw a sight so welcome it made her heart leap in her chest.

"Xpql!" she shouted. He landed with a thud she could feel even from up on her mount, and she sprang from the unicorn and ran to embrace the Dragon. But Xpql did not greet her as she thought he would. The Lalawani, too, seemed so shocked that he lost his power of speech.

Sadie turned from one to the other. Neither seemed to see her as they stared at each other. Then each took a deep breath, and together spit out a single word with equal rancor and venom: "Barbazion!"

17

In the Clutches of the Barbazion

Sadie stared. Beside her, Xpql drew himself up on his hind legs to his full towering height. Black smoke poured from his open nostrils as the Lalawani raised his shield in one hand and his sword in the other. He faced Xpql with a deadly look.

"I will kill you where you stand, Barbazion," he said.

Xpql laughed. "Will you, Barbazion?" he asked. "With what? That little pin? I would like to see you try it, before I turn you into a chattering cinder."

Picker jumped down from his unicorn. "Stop it!" he blazed. "Stop fighting!"

Sadie ran to stand behind him. "That's right!" she cried. "Why are you fighting each other? The real Barbazion are down *there,* in the city!"

Xpql stared at Sadie with bewilderment, but the Lalawani saw his advantage. Stealthily, he ran against the Dragon, driving his sword at Xpql's exposed chest. It happened so quickly that it seemed to unfold in slow motion. Sadie saw the sword go up, and saw the Lalawani step forward, one step, two steps, three steps, and four, and out of the corner of her eye, she saw something move. It was Picker, and he threw himself between the Dragon and the sword, just as the weapon came down. It was as if Sadie were paralyzed. She could only stand there and scream.

"No!" she shrieked. "*No!* Stop! Stop!"

Xpql drew himself up again. He towered above them, ten feet tall, and he blew out a streak of fire. The Lalawani fell back.

"Stop!" Sadie cried, and continued to sob: "Stop, stop, stop, stop, stop!" She fell to her knees over Picker's body, but she could not tell if he was still breathing. Her own hands were shaking so hard she could not even hold them still in front of his face to feel his breath. Seeing her distress, Xpql lowered himself down. His golden eyes narrowed as he stared at the Lalawani. The Lalawani, too, let down his guard. He coughed, twice, to clear Xpql's smoke from his lungs. Then he took up his defiant stance again.

"Give me the children and I will spare your life this time, Barbazion," he said, putting down his sword.

"You, spare *my* life?" Xpql chuckled. "Remember this— it was I who spared *your* life today, Barbazion." And then, without warning, he reached down and snatched the shoulders of Sadie's pajamas with his sharp claws. Grabbing Picker by his clothes as well, he drew in a tremendous breath and took off for the skies.

They landed far from the battle. Xpql dropped Sadie to the ground so he could have two legs to cradle Picker gently down. She fell hard and gasped a little with the pain, but when she saw Picker's face, white and mottled like cottage cheese, she forgot her own hurt and crawled over to him.

"You stand guard, Sadie-Human," Xpql ordered. "I am going to look for an herb to help this one." And then he flew off again.

Sadie knelt beside Picker's body and made herself look at the wound. It was very bloody, and inside the blood she could see the bones of Picker's shoulder. Then she threw up. But Picker was breathing. He didn't look good—he was breathing very fast and very shallowly—but Sadie almost cried out in her relief to know that he was still alive.

"How *could* that Lalawani . . ." she railed. "Why was he fighting Xpql when he could be fighting the Barbazion?" She saw the Lalawani in her mind's eye, his lethal sword in one hand and his beaked helmet in the other—the helmet with the bird's head with the red-rimmed eyes, almost as terrifying as the faces in the catacombs—and her heart sank.

"No . . ." she moaned. "It can't . . ." She shook her head. "Those mummies with the masks, *those* were the Barbazion, that's what Xpql said." But hearing her own words out loud, she realized that although the Egyptians made masks that looked like the corpse in life, perhaps a people might make funeral masks that were instead intended to frighten. "But it can't be . . ." she insisted to Picker, who lay still as death on the ground beside her. "It doesn't make sense. Hanaloni said they saw a Barbazion standing over me in the catacombs, but only Xpql was th—"

A sick, miserable certainty fell over her like a net. "Picker," she whispered. "Do you think it's possible *Barbazion* just means 'enemy'? Could it be possible that the Lalawani could be the Barbazion for the Dragons, and that the Dragons could be the Barbazion for the Lalawani?"

Involuntarily, Sadie remembered the crumbling towers of the Barbazion city. With a pang she understood it had been the Dragons who had been inside. She felt sick to her stomach—utterly betrayed. The Lalawani had made her cheer at the deaths of the Dragons she had sworn to protect, and if she could have, she would have killed them all.

"I hate them!" she cried out bitterly. "I *hate* them—the *Barbazion!*"

"Sadie," Picker whispered. He flinched a little as he tried to talk; he was very pale. "Sadie, do you hear yourself? You just said it—there aren't any Barbazion—there's just the Dragons and the Lalawani. You don't hate Arananu, do you? What about Hanaloni? Are they your enemy now?"

"Yes!" Sadie cried, bursting into tears. "Don't you understand? They're the ones holding Phoebe captive! They *tricked* me—they betrayed me—they hurt you, and . . . and they killed Mrs. Fitz Edna!"

"Yes," said Picker, very quietly, "and the Dragons killed the Lalawani, too. It was the Dragons who did what I saw in the countryside, Sadie. *That* was the Dragons' work—you can't imagine what they did there."

Sadie choked on her tears. "You don't understand," she sobbed. "Mrs. Fitz Edna was a Dragon. *Phoebe* is a Dragon. I can't hate them—I have to hate the Lalawani."

"That's not the only option," Picker whispered.

"You don't understand," Sadie said again, and she hid her face and cried.

"You know," said Picker, so faintly she had to strain to hear him, "when two teams play, it's pretty clear who's playing home and who's playing away, you know?"

"Are you okay, Picker?" Sadie asked, drying her tears and looking at him with concern. "Are you hallucinating?"

"No, no," he said huskily. "It's just this—when people fight good against evil . . ."

"Yeah?"

"It's not like home and away teams, Sadie—people usually think they're on the good side. It's not so clear."

He grimaced then, and winced painfully as the ground shuddered with the force of Xpql's landing. The Dragon grasped a few spiny leaves in one clawed fist, and he peered at

Picker's wound like someone who has had much recent experience in such bloody work. Then he put the spiny leaves in his own mouth, chewed them, and blew scented smoke out onto Picker's wound. Picker moaned and tried to move away, but Xpql kept blowing his hot air on the shoulder. "I must kill the poisons," he explained to Sadie. He looked at the wound again and spat. "How like the Barbazion to strike a child! I am only glad I reached you in time. You, human," he said brusquely to Picker. "Lie still and let the healing do its work."

When he was satisfied, he turned back to Sadie. "I am relieved the Barbazion left you alive," he said tenderly. "I have been looking for you ever since they stole you away from the catacombs. I am astounded that my search succeeded, but as my People say, 'Though life is miserable, it is full of pleasant surprises.'"

"Have you heard anything about my sister?"

"*My* sister has not been moved, as far as we can tell," Xpql replied. "We can only assume she is still within the Glass Castle."

He turned back to Picker and looked at the angry red wound. "Good," he pronounced at last. "But we should not sit here while the enemy is about—we must join the others. Gather some creepers to tie yourself to my back, Sadie-Human. For *you*, I am willing to be a pack animal, because you were with me in my Mountain Time."

Sadie worked like an automaton to make a harness out of

vines to tie her and Picker to the Dragon's back. This time she knew to seat herself towards Xpql's tail, and so she saw the city before they reached it. It pained her to see how it had been reduced to a smoking ruin. All its lovely buildings had been flattened by the Rock-Breakers, and the lush greenery had been scorched by fire. Sadie looked down at it, sick to her stomach, sick that the Lalawani had made her cheer the destruction. She was furious at Arananu and at Hanaloni and at all the Lalawani who had claimed to have rescued Sadie while they had actually been trying to kill Xpql. She caught a whiff of a good familiar smell then, a smell of home, and sniffed deeply. Then she almost threw up again. The smell she had taken for a good one was the smell of roasting meat—the meat that was all that was left of dead Dragons and Lalawani. Behind her, Picker was silent.

They flew past the city towards the woods. Xpql twisted through the sky, turning this way and that to make sure the enemy could not take aim on them. Then Sadie saw a bald spot in the trees, and Xpql began circling down until they touched down into a shadowed glade.

There were nine or ten Dragons there in the clearing. All of them bore the ugly marks of war: great welts on their silvery scales, broken teeth, a missing eye. The oldest of the Dragons hobbled on three legs: the fourth ended in a ragged stump. They hurried over and exclaimed over Xpql, but in a moment, their elation turned back to mourning.

"Where is Shqpl?" Xpql asked the others as soon as he could. "Will she be here soon? Did anyone see Shqpl?"

"I saw her shot by an arrow," one of the Dragons replied. He was missing one of the barbels that hung from his chin and spoke painfully. "She fell on the wall; I cannot imagine she did not break her back."

Xpql bowed his head.

"What about Rsgpt?" he asked the others eagerly.

A different Dragon coughed then and spat out a mouthful of blood. "He was in the towers when they fell. I do not think he got out. Hg was with him, and Xvgt—their fire will not pain them any longer."

"And Hzqgp?"

"Run through with a sword."

And so it went on, name after name, and each time one of the others had seen their comrade die. At each name, Xpql's voice grew quieter, and lower, and he asked his questions more and more slowly, as if he did not want to hear the answer. At last the largest of the Dragons, the one with the missing leg, raised his claw for silence.

"By my account, we are all that is left from the battle," he said, pressing his clawed hand to his heart. "The fire burns painfully at the memory of our comrades. But, as the old saying goes, 'The one-legged creature would be glad for three legs to walk upon.'" He looked down at his wound and smiled grimly. "And it is true. We have been sadly diminished, but we have not been vanquished. The eleven of us here live to fight again—and we eleven will join with others, wherever they are, and avenge those who died in the destruction of Skpbl."

He lowered his head and brought it closer to the others. "The tide will turn for us when we have the Princess Xthpqltthpqlwxn (May Fire and Water Protect Her!) back again. Is that not what the Prophecy foretold? Soon the time will come when we can storm the Glass Castle. With the Princess in our possession, we will be able to rid the planet once and for all of the Barbazion!"

A cry went up from the crowd then, but this time Sadie did not join in. She was staring in horrified fascination at a pile of shining objects in the center of the glade—objects that shimmered in the failing light. It was a pile of wings, and in them Sadie thought she saw a pair that were green and blue, wings that she had often admired on the back of her friend and protector, Hanaloni.

18

The Sacrifice

It was late. Five Dragons stood guard around the glade, each pointing in a different direction towards the blackness of the forest. A few of the others whispered about the glory of battle, but as Sadie stared at their wounds she only saw the ugliness of war. Several times she raised her head and looked at the pile of wings, and it made her want to puke.

Xpql stirred beside her, and Sadie turned to face him.

"You know, Xpql," she whispered. "The Lalawani—the Barbazion, I mean—they don't try to hurt children. When that Lala—Barbazion hit Picker, he was trying to hit *you*."

"Hnnh?" Xpql asked sleepily.

"You said it was like the Barbazion to try to hurt a child," she explained, a lump in her throat. "But we were with the Lala—Barbazion for three days, and they were very kind to us."

"I am sure they are kind to their cattle, too, before they bring them in for the slaughter." Xpql yawned. "Sleep now, Sadie-Human. That is another of our sayings: 'Sleep is a gift that cannot be saved for later.'" He yawned then, and rolled to his side; in a moment, he was snoring.

Sadie didn't bother him again. She looked back over at the sad pile of wings, and felt sick with misery.

Towards midnight, a growl from one of the guards woke her. Around her the Dragons raised their bodies like snakes. Sadie and Picker scrambled to their feet.

"Barbazion!" a voice called from the darkness. Though it was muffled, it was familiar to Sadie's ears. "You are surrounded—if you move, you die. But I did not come to kill you—I came with an offer. Let me speak, and we shall let you live."

"And why should we trust you?" asked the Dragon leader suspiciously. "You do not even show yourself!"

"I will show myself, if you promise not to harm me. If I am killed before my offer is accepted, my warriors will fall on you and kill you all as you stand. Even now my archers have arrows trained on you from every direction." As if in demonstration, an arrow came flying out of darkness into darkness, just above the heads of the Dragons. "Will you let me speak?"

The three-legged Dragon closed his wide eyes and inclined his head, and the speaker came out of the darkness to where the light from the gibbous moon fell on him. It was a Lalawani, dressed in the armor of battle. Two hands came up and pulled off the mask: it was Arananu.

All around him, the Dragons' eyes flickered, and a little murmur went through the crowd.

"I see you know me," declared Arananu. "You know the band I lead, and you know our works. I have killed many of your friends and relatives, and am only sorry I did not succeed in killing each and every one of you. It was I who brought the Rock-Breaker from the northern tribes this morning and used it against your city. But tonight I come to offer myself to you."

He stopped then, and began to unbuckle the heavy armor. He shrugged it off, and held it out towards the Dragon leader before dropping it to the ground with a thud. He stood in front of them, tall and noble, dressed only in the simple clothing of his people, and his long black hair and the black-and-orange wings on his back glinted in the moonlight. Sadie found she hated him and feared for him all at the same time.

"I have come here for a trade, Barbazion," he said. "Let the wingless children go, and you can kill me as you please."

"The children?" the Dragon leader repeated. "Why? Why would you make such a trade?" His eyes narrowed, and he brought his head close to Arananu, examining him closely with a look of deepest suspicion upon his face.

"Because they are my responsibility," Arananu declared. "I was the one who brought them so close to battle, and their lives are on my head. Let them go with my People, and kill me instead."

The Dragon leader stepped forward. "If these two are so important to you," he mused, "perhaps you would be willing to trade the two of them for the one in the Glass Castle."

Arananu shook his head. "I cannot make that deal," he said. "The one in the tower is not mine to barter—the only life I have to trade is my own. Besides, the one in the tower is a matter of war, and this is a matter of love."

"I say we take the deal, Grshxq," one of the other Dragons urged the leader hungrily. "If this Barbazion is stupid enough to offer himself up for sport, I say we add his wings to our collection."

"What does he want with the humans?" asked another. "Perhaps they are worth more than we thought. You, Barbazion," he called out in Lalawani, "why are these humans so valuable to you?"

"They are valuable to me because I love them, and because I owe it to a friend who is now dead," Arananu said. Sadie hung her head; she knew now she had been right about Hanaloni. Tears filled her eyes, but Arananu went on. "Perhaps you do not understand love, Barbazion, I do not know. But we Lalawani know love and we know honor—and it is my honor to die out of love for their safety. Do you accept my offer?"

The Dragons conferred. At last Grshxq waddled over to Arananu. The Lalawani stood very still as he stared into the Dragon's enormous face. At last Grshxq reached up and pulled out a hair from Arananu's beard. The Lalawani did not flinch, even when the Dragon blew out a thin stream of fire and incinerated the hair. He spoke in a low voice to Arananu, but Sadie, standing close, could hear it: "You will die slowly, Barbazion—and we will enjoy watching your suffering."

Arananu's face did not change. The nobility and courage there were beautiful; he was beautiful. Sadie's heart hurt.

"Then you accept my offer?" he asked.

"We do."

"No!" shouted Xpql. "We should not trade the Sadie-Human, not even for this prize. We . . ."

"No," agreed another voice. The Dragons turned. It was Picker. He had come to stand between Arananu and the leader of the Dragons. "I don't accept the offer—I won't go." He turned to Arananu. "I won't accept your life for mine."

"I won't go, either," Sadie cried, leaping forward and taking Picker's hand for strength. "We won't leave here. But don't kill him. Let him go!"

Xpql was at her side, too, but he did not make a declaration. Instead, he whispered in her ear. "Wait, Sadie-Human. If the Barbazion really trust you as an ally, you may be the best hope of rescuing the Princess. I urge you, go!"

Sadie thought of Phoebe, alone up in the castle. She had to get Phoebe back—that was plain—and Xpql was right that it would be easier to do that with the Lalawani who held her sister captive than with the Dragons. And, she thought, maybe she could find some way to convince them all to stop the fighting once she had Phoebe back. An embryonic idea began to form in her head, but she was not sure if it was a brilliant plan or the feeble sort of thing you make up when you are playing spies on a hot summer day, rules for a game that will be over soon, anyway, when the call goes out for dinner.

"Children," Arananu entreated. "The Protector will take care of me. Go, *please,* if you love me. Go!"

Picker shook his head stubbornly, but Sadie stepped forward.

"Look," she said, "as you keep saying, I'm just a child, and I'm beginning to think I'm a pretty stupid one at that. But I once read on Earth that when two groups were fighting, they would make a trade of hostages. I say Arananu stays here— alive!—but Xpql and I will go to the Lalawani—to the Barbazion—and we will stay there—alive!—until we meet again."

"Why?" asked Grshxq. "Why would we want this creature, this Barbazion, if we cannot kill him?"

His question was echoed by a Lalawani, calling out from the dark of the forest. "Why should we take a Barbazion into our camp? Can we use him to replace the beasts he killed? What say you, Barbazion? Can you already feel the bit between your teeth?"

"Because!" Sadie said, talking fast and thinking faster. "Because this war is going nowhere. It's . . . it's taking too long, all these raids and surprise attacks. I say you meet once and for all in front of the Glass Castle, and have a final battle. But the battle does not start until the hostages are returned and I give the command myself. Do you agree? No one fights until *I* give the word."

Picker was staring at her as if she had gone crazy, and Sadie wondered if she had. She looked around the moonlit glade at the Dragons, and tried to peer into the darkness to see the Lalawani that were hidden there. Then she thought she was better off playing with dolls than with people's lives. *But after all*, she told herself, *they'll be trying to kill each other whether I'm here or not, and who knows? Maybe my plan will work.*

"I came here to offer my life," said Arananu, "but I think Sadu's plan is a good one. Let us have our one last battle. It is time for us to end this war in victory."

One of the Dragons laughed then, sending out a tongue of fire to lick the air next to Arananu's ear. The battle scars on his back were ugly, but the hatred in his eyes was uglier still. "Yes," he said. "I, too, long for victory." He turned to Sadie. "Well, human," he said, "yours is a strange plan, but perhaps not a bad one. But how will we ensure that the Barbazion do not kill Xpql?"

"Because you will not kill Arananu," Sadie answered promptly. "When we all meet in front of the Glass Castle, you will see that they have kept their word, and they will see that you have kept yours."

"In other words," the young Dragon drawled, "if Xpql is not there, we will slowly rip this Barbazion from limb to wing, wing to limb."

The three-legged Dragon, Grshxq, came up to Sadie. "You want us to gather for one final battle," he said in Dragon. "Why?"

"Because I'm hoping you won't need to fight it," Sadie stammered.

"Ah," said the Dragon, nodding wisely. "I see—you will work to make sure they are all dead when we arrive."

"Not exactly," Sadie corrected, "but promise me this, please—when you get there, promise me your people will not attack until I give the sign."

"I do not know why I trust you," the old Dragon sighed. "Perhaps it is because you look so much like the Princess (May Fire and Water Protect Her!). Or it may be that I am growing sentimental in my old age. I hope it is not our undoing. I will trust you, human, though I may live to regret it. Our lives are in your hands."

Sadie was still shuddering when Picker approached her. "What are you doing?" he asked her nervously.

"I'm not really sure," she whispered. "But I'm hoping we can get to Phoebe, and I can return her to the Dragons without a fight, and then we can convince everyone that war is not the answer."

Xpql rolled his eyes. "*This* is the plan to which I'm trusting my life?" he snorted. "I can only hope your strategy will take more shape soon. At the moment, it seems like the cobwebs the attercops weave: pretty, but full of holes. My plan was simpler. It did not involve a great and final battle when our greatest weapon is firmly in the hands of the enemy."

"Don't worry," Sadie said. "We have a saying, 'Necessity is the mother of invention.'"

"We have a saying, too," Xpql replied. "'He who follows a fool is a fool.'" He sighed. "Well, I am a fool—I follow you."

They started to walk away, but Picker leaned forward and grabbed Sadie by the shoulder of her pajamas. Then he leaned forward and gave her the briefest and tightest of hugs. "I'll do what I can here to make your plan work," he said. "But seriously, Sadie—take care of yourself. I'm counting on seeing you again, with Phoebe at your side."

"That's why I'm doing this," she said. And then, "Hey, Picker—be safe."

She walked up to Arananu. The Lalawani stared at her, his brown eyes large and warm. There was a nobility and resignation in him that made Sadie want to cry. She still hated him—he had betrayed her, making her trust him when he was trying to kill her friends. He was a Barbazion, a bloodthirsty butcher, and he had turned her into a bloodthirsty butcher, too—and for that she could never forgive him. But at the same time, a part of her ached for him, and remembered the way he had smiled at her so tenderly when they first met in the tent. She saw a glimpse of the fear and pain in his eyes now, and the full force of his sacrifice fell upon her. On Earth, they said there was no greater love than to lay down your life for your friends, and that's what Arananu was doing now: offering his life for that of a child he barely knew.

She blinked; the tears were pricking behind her eyelids. "Thank you," she stammered, and though she still thought she hated him, she meant it. Then she turned and walked into the dark shadows of the trees, with Xpql following behind.

19

The Gathering

There were big holes in the Lalawani caravan now, holes as painfully obvious as missing teeth. There was no play with the torches, and no lighthearted songs. The Lalawani wailed and beat on drums as they marched.

Xpql was unmoved by the sad sound. "You see," he muttered to Sadie, "that was what I was telling you: their stench is unbelievable. And the noise! If I have to listen to it for one more minute, I will bite off my own ears."

"They're sad!" Sadie snapped. She thought of Hanaloni, and she thought of Mrs. Fitz Edna, and she knew she could not stand any more grief. "They sing because they're sad!"

Xpql considered this. "Perhaps it is a happier sound than I thought," he mused. He let loose a great billowing cloud of sulfurous smoke then, and several of the Lalawani who walked near them moved even farther away.

Sadie sighed. It was very exhausting to be rescued twice in one day and still not know whether she was in the hands of friends or enemies. Finally she turned to Xpql, addressing him in Lalawani so the others would not be suspicious.

"Tell me," she demanded, "why do you fight these people?"

Xpql stared at her in surprise. "How can you ask that?" he asked in Dragon. "You yourself saw what the Barbazion did to the river, and to the mountain, and to those in the watchtower. You saw what they did in Skpbl, not to mention what they did to my sister and my grandmother. How can you ask why we fight them?"

Sadie pondered this, and then she looked around for a Lalawani she knew. She saw one, far from Xpql. It was Olani, the one who had confessed her fear to Sadie in the tent, back when things had seemed much simpler.

"Can I ask you a question?" she asked, touching the Lalawani's sleeve.

"Certainly, Sadu," Olani replied. "I will try to answer if it is not too difficult." She was a little stiff in her manner, and Sadie knew it was because she alone had seen the terror behind Olani's fierceness.

"Why do the Lalawani fight the Dra—the Barbazion?"

"Why do we fight?" repeated Olani with a harsh laugh. "*You* who were captured by them should know why. But I will answer with a question: Why does the djinalane run away from the hawk when it circles above? We fight for survival. The Barbazion do not want to share the world with us. If we do not fight, we die, and fighting is preferable to dying, in my opinion."

Sadie thought about that for a while.

"If the Barbazion stopped attacking you, would you stop fighting?"

"If the Barbazion stopped attacking us, we would be foolish to wait for the moment they decided to attack us again. That is the way of things, Sadu. There will be no safety until they are dead, each and every one of them."

"But what if they promised to stop fighting?"

"Who would trust the promise of a Barbazion? It is a trusting man who trusts the promises of a friend, and a gullible fool who trusts the promises of his enemies. No, Sadie, the fighting will only end when they are all dead."

"I just don't understand how it started," Sadie sighed, looking up to the moon for guidance. The eye, misshapen like a rotten orange, looked down at her impassively, shining down on the places where the dead Lalawani should have been walking.

"Does it matter?" asked Olani with a philosophical shrug. "If we stop to consider how it all began, the Barbazion would kill us while we stood around with our mouths open, wondering. The Barbazion have always been there, like a demon of the sun, killing our people. Then came the Prophecy. . . ."

"The Prophecy?"

"The Prophecy of peace. It said that the Protector would bring the blessings of night during the day, and at that time there would be one born who would bring peace to our world. It said that one would be born of a golden egg—born wingless like a Barbazion animal, but two-legged, like a person. And the Prophecy said that the Wingless One would have unspeakable power. Whoever had her in an army of ten would command an army of ten thousand. And it was true. At first, after her birth, the Barbazion struck at us like a mighty fist, and our blood ran out in rivers. But we knew that if we pleased the Protector by recapturing the one who belonged with the People, her power would be ours. And since we reclaimed her, *we* have been the ones to let loose the torrents."

Sadie's heart sank. Her ill-considered plan was, as Xpql said, insubstantial and full of holes. The best plan she could muster was a naïve attempt to bring the remaining Lalawani and Dragons together, to force them to see how terribly diminished their numbers were, to show them that the uneasy peace of the past was preferable to the slaughter that was to come. But now she wondered. Fear is a terrible goad towards violence, and underneath it all, every Lalawani and each of the Dragons was miserable with fear. She could not imagine anything that would keep such frightened people from fighting.

"But the moment of victory is at hand," Olani went on, misinterpreting Sadie's unhappy silence. "The messengers have already gone out to the other tribes. Soon ten thousand Lalawani will gather on the plain before the Glass Castle."

"Ten thousand?" Sadie exclaimed. "That many!"

"Ten thousand," Olani repeated. "And not one of us will stop until every last child of the Barbazion is dead."

Miserably, Sadie saw that Olani spoke the truth. As they walked on through the night, other tribes of Lalawani joined them, like tributaries to great rivers that pour relentlessly towards the sea. As each new group arrived, they came to stand before Xpql, to spit into his eyes and heap abuse upon him. Sadie ached for him. He was panting, trying to hide his weakness, but Sadie knew from her long trek with him how hard it was for him to keep up at their pace. His face was drawn with effort, and his breath came out in short, quick puffs. Now and again he coughed, and smiled sardonically as the Lalawani around him jumped out of the way of the flames that shot from his mouth. Sadie wondered if he was still frightened, now that he was surrounded by the Barbazion of his nightmares. But like Arananu, he had arranged his face in a mask of arrogance and bravery.

The Lalawani kept on coming. Sadie walked alongside the others, swept along in the great river away from Xpql. The Lalawani were tall, and beside them, Sadie had the unpleasant feeling of having shrunk down. It made her feel like a child lost in the supermarket, searching among the legs for her mother. She had not felt like a child since she had seen the dammed-up waters that had drowned the city of Xthltg.

What was I thinking, that I could end this war by myself? she thought unhappily. *Delusional, that's what I was. Ten thou-*

sand Lalawani! They'll massacre the Dragons, and it will all be my fault!

But then, at the end of a weary day of marching, Sadie saw signs that the massacre might not be as one-sided as she had thought. Towards dusk, a black cloud rose up in the south, whistling like an angry wind. The Lalawani stopped and murmured; the archers reached for their arrows. The cloud was approaching—it blocked the setting sun. The Lalawani turned to one another, and Sadie could hear the fear in their murmurs. Then the cloud was upon them, lit up with jets of fire, and from ahead in the crowd, Xpql sent up a cry of triumph that nearly singed his guards.

It was the Dragons—hundreds of them, maybe thousands, flying high, speeding north towards the Glass Castle. All the rest of that afternoon, the marching Lalawani stopped to watch other bands of Dragons come streaking through the sky. Even at night, flashes of light lit up the darkness, and Sadie knew that the great migration went on. Around her, the Lalawani were still talking about the upcoming battle. Now that they no longer seemed so sure of victory, Sadie heard in their voices a different kind of courage—a courage born out of desperation. It was die fighting or die running, and only in fighting was there a hope of life. Sadie's heart hurt in her chest. There was going to be a final battle, all right, far worse than she had ever imagined, and there was nothing she could do about it. The martial beat of the marching Lalawani rang in her ears like the heartbeat of an enormous monster, and she could barely hear herself think. She began to feel frantic—frantic with exhaustion and fear. Tears began to stream down her cheeks. To her humiliation, she found she was wailing.

Olani fought her way through the crowd. Putting her slender arms around Sadie's shoulders, she spoke soothingly: "Don't despair, Sadu! We're so near to victory that I can taste it!"

She spoke quickly, with shining eyes, not understanding that her words were like hot pokers to Sadie's ears. It was all too much—too much. Sadie fell to her knees in the middle of that great horde. Olani tried to lift her to her feet.

"She's been traumatized by her experience!" she called out to the others, not without truth. "Oh, I could *kill* the Barbazion who did this to her!" Her eyes flashed fiercely, and she looked back towards Xpql as if she would have liked to tear him limb from limb. Sadie remembered the look she had seen on Olani's face back in the tent, when she'd dipped the arrows into the poison. That look was back on her face as the Lalawani strode up to Xpql, her red-and-gold wings streaming out behind her. She reached over her shoulder and pulled out a black-tipped arrow and held it over Xpql like a dagger.

"You, Barbazion!" she addressed him, her voice quivering with anger or fear. "I command you to carry this child."

Xpql let out a sulfurous expletive at that, and Sadie, remembering how he had told her he would never be a beast of burden for the Lalawani, shrank back, "No . . . no . . ." she protested weakly to Olani. The Lalawani turned swiftly back towards Sadie. Kneeling before her, she cupped the child's face in her gentle hands.

"Don't be afraid, Sadu," she soothed. "I will walk beside you and ensure the beast does not harm you." Still, Sadie shook her head. Her eyes had filled with tears again as she looked at Xpql, miserably hemmed in by his enemies. Then the Dragon inclined his head, slowly, as if assenting. His golden eyes were full of pity, and Sadie saw he understood she did not wish to humiliate him. She let Olani lead her on rubbery legs towards the Dragon, and once more she climbed upon his broad back, laying her head on the smooth scales of his neck. Olani walked beside her, her hand on Sadie's weary shoulders, and there, sandwiched between Barbazion of both stripes, each believing they were the one protecting the girl, Sadie slept.

20

The Glass Castle

Towards the dawn of the second day, Sadie saw something poking up over the edge of the horizon: a little spike, too square and regular to be anything but a building. By the time the great throng finally stopped to rest at noon, the tower was taller than Sadie's hand at the end of her outstretched arm.

"It's the Glass Castle," she said, and no one contradicted her.

So there it was, Phoebe's prison, an enormous tower of obsidian glass, balanced on the top of a huge outcropping of striated rock. For a moment, Sadie's heart leapt to be so close to her goal, but as she looked around at the teeming hordes of Lalawani around her, and thought of the Dragons twisting their way through the air towards the battle, she knew she was as far from rescuing her sister as ever.

"Phoebe . . ." she whispered. Her arms ached to hold her sister, to gaze upon that lovable face, and her eyes filled with tears as she looked at the tower, standing tall and defiant and unspeakably frightening with its roving red light circling at the top.

She did not feel better when they came to the base of the plateau where the tower stood. The great crowd behind her grew silent as the shadow of the tower fell upon them, and every eye was on a strange shape that was winding down the curved path down the plateau's sides. It came closer, and closer still, and then Sadie could tell what it was. It was a Dragon, a bit pulling back the corners of her broad mouth, a set of reins holding up her head so high she could barely see where to put her feet. A fat Lalawani sat on her back, the reins gripped brutally in one massive hand, and he drove the Dragon right in front of the assembled multitude to where Sadie waited with Olani and the leaders of the Lalawani tribes.

As the Dragon drew close, Xpql shuddered so viciously that Sadie almost fell from his back. When she looked at the captive Dragon, she understood Xpql's rage. Blinders covered the Dragon's golden eyes, and great red welts ran down her sides. Without a word, Sadie slipped from Xpql's back. She wanted to scream at them all that Xpql was a free Dragon, a person and not a beast to be ridden, but she said nothing. The fat Lalawani was drawing closer. When he came to a halt before them, the Lalawani leaders bowed deeply. Here and there a cheer went up out of the crowd.

"It is Hlavanu," Olani whispered to Sadie. "The leader of all the tribes. To think I am seeing him with my own eyes . . ."

Hlavanu looked over to her, an eyebrow raised, like a teacher who waits for the class to be silent. Olani withered under his disapproval, and then Hlavanu moved his Dragon closer to Xpql. The two Dragons turned their heads; the mutual shame of their meeting burned in their downcast eyes.

Hlavanu held out his hand to Sadie.

"The messengers brought me word of your plan, Wingless One," he said, appraising her. "The Protector smiles on us, indeed, sending us such good counselors."

He turned to the others.

"It is as you have heard," he said to those in earshot. "The Barbazion will meet us here on the plains, the same plains where our ancestors slew the monsters of the sun a hundred generations ago. Spread among the tribes and tell them: the battle will begin soon. The enemy approaches!" The closest Lalawani all nodded and slipped back into the crowd. The effect was like the waves pulling back into the sea: in a moment, Sadie was left alone before Hlavanu, with only Xpql and Olani beside her. The Dragon snorted out an impatient burst of smoke, as if asking Sadie to make her next move, but

Sadie had no next move to make. Desperately, she tried to pull together the strands of the idea she had had in the woods, the plan that would rescue Phoebe and stop the Barbazion war forever, but there was no plan. She looked up at the tower and sighed.

Hlavanu caught the sound, and cupped his hand under her chin.

"Poor child," he said. "You have suffered so—and yet, as those of Arananu's tribe inform me, we owe you so much. Is there anything we can do to ease your pain?"

"No," Sadie answered, feeling that nothing would ever ease her pain again. As if upbraiding her for not answering, Xpql let out a little tongue of fire. Sadie looked at him helplessly.

"Come, Sadu of Arananu's tribe," said Hlavanu, ignoring the Dragon entirely. "Come ride with me." Two other Lalawani came forward and lifted Sadie in front of Hlavanu on his Dragon. Sadie sent Xpql a panicked look, but Hlavanu jerked up the reins viciously and turned the Dragon towards the mountain. The Glass Castle rose up above them, impossibly large, and still Sadie had no idea what she was going to do.

"Our people did not always live in the desert," Hlavanu was saying as he drove the Dragon into the courtyard on top of the plateau. He gestured towards the plains below them. "When the Lalawani first fell to this planet from the stars, they lived here, among plenty. It was green and fertile, this land, until the demons of the sun came with their fire. That is what the songs say. The demons of the sun came and drove the Lalawani away from the fertile lands to where the life is harsh and hard in the desert. But then, hiding from the heat of the day and seeking the cool of the night, the Lalawani found the Protector. And now the Protector has led us back here. The Prophecy has been very clear: when the Wingless One that came from the golden egg has been returned to the people of the Protector, the Lalawani will defeat their enemies in final battle. Then we will return to our ancestral lands, to make them green and fertile once more. And you, Sadu of Arananu's tribe, you are like the Lalawani. You have suffered under the Barbazion, but survived until morning, and you have ridden your enemy triumphantly back to our ancestral city, praise be the Protector. Soon you will stand here, overlooking the field of battle, and see the moment that we triumph over the Barbazion."

Sadie didn't answer that. She looked up at the tower, with its searching red light, and sighed.

"Poor child," Hlavanu whispered again. "Is there *anything* that will ease your heart?"

Then Sadie realized what Xpql had wanted her to say, back when she had stood next to him on the plain before Hlavanu.

"Yes," she answered. "There is. I want to see the one in the tower—the other Wingless One—the one who looks like me."

The guards at the tower's door moved apart to let them in. Three Lalawani sat there in the tower's large foyer, each with a hand lazily wrapped around the handle of a mug. When they saw Hlavanu, they stopped talking, flushed, and jumped to their feet.

"This is Sadu, sent by the Protector to ensure our victory," Hlavanu explained to them. "She was with Arananu's band when they destroyed the city of the towers, and those who know her tell me she has come to help us destroy the enemy once and for all. But first she is here to see the one in the tower. Escort her up to the Wingless One. She is to visit for ten minutes, and then I will need her back once more."

Slowly, stiffly, he bowed to Sadie. "I hope your visit is a good one, Sadu," he said. "I will see you soon, and you will explain to me this plan to obliterate the enemy."

Sadie's heart sank. *Well, what did you expect?* she reproved herself. *Did you think they were just going to hand Phoebe over to you?* Well, yes: that is just what she had hoped, stupid though that was. She was about to upbraid herself for her idiocy when a terrible sound came from above. Four pairs of eyes, three Lalawani and one human, flew up to the ceiling.

"It is the Wingless One," the tallest guard explained to Sadie. "*This* is the sort of concert to which she treats us daily."

Sadie hardly heard him. She knew that sound: it was Phoebe in what their father always called "a full grand mal tantrum." A smile broke over her face before she could stop it. She might not know how she going to get Phoebe out of that tower, and she might not know how she was going to stop the war and find Picker and convince a Dragon to carry the three of them back to suburban Earth through the Portal, but the fact remained that she had made it nearly to her goal. She, Sadie Ann Guthrie, had gone through a Portal, over the perils of desert and sea, through fire and ice, and here she was, only a hundred feet away from her sister.

The glorious sound of Phoebe's cry had faded away to echoes. The three Lalawani guards sat back down at their table. One reached forward and picked up the small bones that lay there: they were gambling. Sadie smiled—she was gambling, too.

"Can I go upstairs?" she asked.

"Go upstairs?" one of the guards repeated incredulously. "I thought the fat old man was joking."

"Here—hand me the bones," another ordered. "If I win, you two escort her. I have had enough of the Wingless One for today." He held up a bandaged finger and waved it ruefully. "I tell you," he said to Sadie, "I have faced the Barbazion three times in battle and each time triumphed without a scratch. This assignment here was supposed to be a reward for my valor, and it is *here* that I am wounded on a daily basis. I advise you not to go up there—that wingless demon bites, and she bites hard."

"I know," said Sadie, grinning, "but I'll take the risk."

"Come, then," said the third, jerking his head towards the stairs. Sadie ran past him, taking the stairs two at a time, the guard puffing behind her. A little light fell onto the curving steps from above, and Sadie hurried, hoping it was Phoebe's room. But it was only a slit cut into the obsidian, and a Lalawani warrior standing there, an arrow aimed out the window.

"Who is this?" she asked suspiciously, looking from Sadie to the guard. "Where is she going?"

"Hlavanu sent her up to see the prisoner," the guard replied, catching his breath. The Lalawani stared at Sadie in blank amazement.

"You don't want to go up there!" she said to Sadie. "You have no idea how the Wingless One scratches!"

But Sadie did have an idea, and she sprang up the stairs with renewed vigor, until she was forced to pause for breath, her hand on her hammering heart. A voice surprised her; she looked up. Another guard was staring at her.

"Who are you? Where are you going?"

"Up to see the prisoner."

"Why would you want to see her?" the guard asked, unconsciously rubbing a shin with the sole of his other foot. "She is small, but she kicks like a devil." He gave a surprised look at Sadie's smile, but let her past. And then Sadie was up the stairs again, always higher, always towards her goal.

A familiar sound was coming from upstairs now—an arrhythmic thumping, as if someone were lying on the floor and kicking her feet at a door. Sadie smiled more, and she ran up that last flight of stairs three at a time.

Another Lalawani guard stood there, close to a door. She, too, stared at Sadie with surprise, and then past Sadie to the solider who came panting up behind her.

"Hlavanu has given this one ten minutes with the prisoner," he said.

"You had better take my helmet, then," the guard said to Sadie, shaking her head. "That monster in there pulls hair like a wild thing."

"I know," said Sadie. "But I'll take the risk."

The guard reached down, took a key from her waist, and turned it in the lock. The door opened a crack, only to be slammed shut again.

"Phoebe!" Sadie whispered in English. "Open the door! It's me! It's Sadie!"

The door opened with a wondering creak, and Phoebe's tear-streaked face appeared in the crack. She looked disheveled and not a little bit wild, but she was Phoebe all right, down to the pout. This was her sister, and Sadie was decidedly happy to see her.

"Come on, Phoebe," she said. "I'm here to bring you home."

21

King Solomon

There are some things sweeter in the doing than in the telling: that too-short reunion was one of them. Sadie flung herself to her knees and embraced her sister, kissing that sweet face over and over again, until at last that tangle of arms and teary faces sorted themselves out to be Phoebe sitting on Sadie's lap, her arms around her sister's neck, holding on so tight it seemed she would never let go.

"Let's go home, Sadie!" she sobbed.

"I wish we could," Sadie whispered. "I really do, Pheebs, but we only have ten minutes and then . . ."

Suddenly she looked up. The light was failing outside the tower. Disentangling herself from her sister, Sadie ran to where the obsidian wall had been scraped thin to make a window. Outside the door she heard the guards calling to one another, clattering down the stairs as they exclaimed at the sight.

"What is it?" asked Phoebe.

"It's the Dragons," Sadie answered. "The Dragons are here at last." She tried to hide her sinking dread from her sister, and Phoebe leapt to her feet. "Come on, Sadie!" she cried. "They'll take us home to Daddy and Mama! Come *on!* What are you waiting for?"

Sadie tried to stop her before she opened the door, but when Phoebe wanted to, she could be quick. She wrenched the door open, and Sadie saw that the guards were gone. All was silent in the hall.

Sadie gave a last glance out the window. The dark forest that stretched behind the tower rock was obscured by the fiery cloud of Dragons. She sighed.

"All right, Phoebe," she said. "We're going. But be *quiet.*"

Hoping that Phoebe had miraculously learned the value of silence in her captivity, Sadie tiptoed down the curving stair. Her heart pounded in her chest so hard it made her dizzy, and she had to stop now and then just to keep from slipping. They came around a corner to another abandoned window, and Sadie stared out.

Down below, it appeared that every Lalawani on that planet was amassed on the plains in front of the tower rock.

Not too far away from them, a mass of Dragons was gathering. The sky was still black with the thousands more that were spinning through the air, and they landed on the ground like locusts falling on the corn. The two armies were not too close—there was a space between them about the width of an arrow's flight, or a spurt of Dragon flame. They stood there, expectant, and the weight of their waiting crushed down on Sadie. Apparently, ridiculously, both sides had agreed to her outrageous request that they not begin the battle until Sadie herself gave the word.

"Come on, Phoebe," she said, sighing. Taking her sister firmly by the hand, she hurried down the rest of the stairs.

"Where are you going?" one of the guards shouted as they came into the room with the abandoned gaming table.

"Didn't you know?" Sadie asked him. "Hlavanu is waiting for me down there. The battle can't start until I give the order."

Her voice rang with authority, because what she said was true. The guard stared at her, and then he bowed his head.

"I do not envy you that destiny," he said. "But I trust the Protector. If you have the courage to walk with the Wingless One, then I will find the courage to walk with you. We will go to Hlavanu together."

He bowed, then, and helped Sadie and her sister down the narrow steps and through the front door. Phoebe blinked painfully in the sunshine, and hid her face, but Sadie stood there, eyes open without seeing what she should do. The forest stretched out behind them, like a welcome invitation of safety, but even if Sadie could have escaped their guard and abandoned the Lalawani and the Dragons to their battle, she could not leave Picker—and even if she could have left Picker, she knew she would not be able to escape that planet without help. Her brain spun madly, thinking of ways to convince the Dragons to take them home, but it spun without purpose, like the wheels of a car stuck in the mud. But then she saw movement on the plain, and it drove all thoughts of a plan out of her mind.

Something was moving into the empty space between the two armies. It was a Dragon—the Dragon that carried Hlavanu on its back. Another Dragon came out to meet them, a free Dragon, limping on three intact limbs with the slow dignity of its race. It was Grshxq, and he wore a strange frill around his neck, a frill made of wings that sparkled in light of the sun. He shook his head a little, setting the wings to shimmering, and faced Hlavanu with defiance. It was then that an arrow came flying out of the assembled Lalawani towards the Dragons.

Sadie cried out: she knew in a second that it was all over. The shot would fly into the Dragons, and the Dragons would respond in kind, and that arrow would be the beginning of a battle that would end in death and suffering. If she could have jumped down and stopped the arrow with her own body, she would have done it, but Phoebe was there, pulling at her hand, and she yanked Sadie away from the edge. Then Sadie saw, miraculously, that the arrow had fallen short, and that Grshxq had held up his forefoot to hold back the Dragons behind him. He had remembered his promise to Sadie to wait until she had arrived, and he had stopped the attack. Sadie sighed in relief: the battle had not yet started. It could still be averted. More quickly, she led her sister and their guard down the steep track to the plain.

They were still far away when Hlavanu and Grshxq saw them coming. The Lalawani leader raised his hand as he recognized Sadie and her guard, and then the crowds behind Hlavanu parted. Another Dragon limped out of the Lalawani camp, and with a pang Sadie saw it was Xpql. He had a heavy yoke across his neck, and a Lalawani on his back. Even through the thick smoke that surrounded him, Sadie could see the flaming of his eyes. Her heart ached to see him this way, and she longed to tear the iron collar off him. Then Picker came out of the smoky air that surrounded the Dragons, bringing Arananu with him by the hand. Arananu was still alive, but just barely—Sadie could see he had been terribly abused. One wing hung crookedly down his back in tatters, and his eyes seemed to be swollen shut. He stumbled as Picker led him, he who strode through the Lalawani camps with such strength and freedom! Sadie felt a rising rage at all of them.

Hlavanu got off his mount then. He went over to Arananu and covered first Arananu's eyes and then his own with his hand. Then he turned and called out to the Lalawani army behind him. Sadie heard his voice, though not his words, and then she gasped again. The Lalawani army was parting, and something was coming through.

Sadie stared. It was an enormous animal, much bigger than the unicorns, a winged animal, with a leonine head surrounded by a glorious mane. It towered above Dragons and Lalawani, and when it shook its great black-feathered wings, the banners of the Lalawani snapped as if in a heavy wind. Sadie had never seen anything like him. Or maybe she had— she thought of the great black shapes that wheeled across the face of the moon, back when she was with Xpql in the desert. And now that free creature was here, captive, and as it drew close Sadie saw that a Lalawani rode on its back, something oval cradled in her arms.

Then Hlavanu gave a command, and the Lalawani dug her heels into the creature's sides, once, twice, her spurs drawing black blood. The creature reared, and then stretched out its tremendous wings, twenty feet across, and flapped them in a fury. Even as far away as they were, Sadie's hair blew back as if she were in a storm, and one of the wings that had been fastened around Grshxq's neck flew up and blew over the plain. Then the creature was in the air, spurred on by the Lalawani on its back. Every eye was upon it as it rose into the sky. It sped through the air faster than a hawk, faster than an eagle, sniffing at the clouds, and then it was gone. Everyone gasped then, and sighed as it reappeared through what looked like a hole in the sky.

"It's the Portal," Sadie groaned to Phoebe. "They know about the Portal."

The animal disappeared again, and then reappeared, and then, with a blinding flash, it was gone. There was a tremendous crash, and Sadie cried out with all the others. "The Rock-Breaker!" she whispered. "They used the Rock-Breaker on the Portal. . . ."

The Dragons seemed to have the same idea. At a call from Grshxq, three Dragons rose up into the air, twisting and turning like fish swimming through a river, until they reached the place where the Portal had been. Though they darted this way and that, they did not disappear.

"It's gone," Sadie breathed.

"Yes," said the guard beside her. "It is gone. The Barbazion will never be able to take our Wingless One away again."

Sadie felt Phoebe's hand gripping her own and realized she could not explain it to her sister. She could not tell her that they were trapped in Dragonland forever.

But if Phoebe didn't understand, she was the only one on that plain who didn't. As the guard led them to the place where Grshxq and Hlavanu stood, Sadie heard both armies muttering. But then she was standing in the space between the two armies, the guard had disappeared from her side, and both Dragons and Lalawani were gazing at Phoebe with such naked hunger that it made Sadie decidedly nervous.

"Sadu, my child," said Hlavanu, slowly advancing towards them, "why did you take the prisoner from the tower?"

Sadie had not thought about how she was going to answer that question. It was not that her plan was full of holes, but rather that she had no plan at all. But still she tossed back her matted hair defiantly and looked at the Dragons and at the Lalawani, and she answered them with the truth.

"I took her because she is my sister," she said.

Grshxq growled then. "She is not your sister," he corrected. "You had no right to endanger her here. She is one of the People, and does not belong to you or yours, but to us and ours." He moved towards her, staring at Sadie with his gold hypnotic eyes, and for a moment she forgot where she was.

"Xthpqltthpqlwxn," Grshxq said softly to Phoebe, "we are here to take you back, little daughter."

He moved towards her, and Sadie felt Phoebe's little hand loosen in her own and begin to pull away. Her heart sank. For all that Phoebe *was* her sister, she was also a Dragon, and maybe she would choose to stay there with the moongrass and the pools of Frthgl and the Dragons who treated her like a princess. But Phoebe looked from the Dragons to the Lalawani and back to Sadie, and she stepped forward and fed her small hand into her sister's. She squeezed Sadie's hand tightly, as if trying to make their two hands one. And then she made a declaration.

"I want to go home to Mama and Daddy," she said.

Sadie let out a breath of relief, but Hlavanu jumped forward.

"The Wingless One is not yours," he asserted, throwing out his chest. "Our songs have long sung of the golden egg child who would come to us from the Protector and bring us victory—our claims to this creature are ancient."

"Not as ancient as ours," Grshxq hissed quietly. "*We* have sung songs of the one who would come from the golden egg for a thousand years. She is *our* hope of victory, promised to *us*."

"Wait!" Sadie cried out. "You both want her because she will bring you victory, but I want her because I *love* her. That makes my claim the strongest!"

The others only laughed at this speech.

"Perhaps in *your* world desire makes a claim strong," Grshxq said, "but here it is blood that matters."

"And prophecy," put in Hlavanu. He and Grshxq were both advancing towards the two girls. Hlavanu was closer, and he reached out towards them. With dismay, Sadie saw he was not extending the hand of friendship: he held a long curved knife in his hand.

Sadie sprang back. She was thinking as hard as she could, but after all, she was only a child of eleven, and not even the smartest kid she knew. The smartest kid she knew was Picker, but he was just standing there watching, and was no help at all. She thought of all the smart people she knew: her parents, Albert Einstein, Marie Curie, Shakespeare . . . and then she thought of King Solomon, the wisest man in the Bible.

Suddenly she knew what to do. Hlavanu still stretched out his hand with the knife, but Sadie had her own knife from Hanaloni. She whipped it out now, whispered into her sister's hair, and held the knife to Phoebe's waist.

"Since neither of you will agree that my sister belongs wholly to the other," she said, her voice ringing out over the plain, "will each of you agree to settle for half?"

Hlavanu considered; Grshxq considered; Arananu considered; Picker stared; Xpql closed his eyes as if in pain. Then Hlavanu said, "With the Wingless One dead, neither side would be assured of victory. We could go back to the way it was before the day the sun was blotted from the sky. Yes," he said wisely, "I would assent to that agreement."

Grshxq bowed his head. "You are indeed wise," he said to Sadie. "At first, in the forest, I was suspicious, but now I see your plan has merit after all. I accede to your proposal. Kill Xthpqltthpqlwxn—May Fire and Water Protect Her."

"*What?*" Sadie burst out. "I don't believe this!" But believe it or not, Hlavanu and Grshxq were nodding to show they agreed to Sadie's proposal, and with Xpql and Arananu, they moved forward slowly, to show they would help her carry it out. Sadie just stood there, mouth open, bemused, befuddled, and bewildered, watching them come. But then Picker jumped forward. He let out a piercing whistle, and suddenly there was a flash of brightness, a streak of white that came running out over the plain. It happened so quickly that neither Dragons nor Lalawani had time to respond before Picker was helping Sadie onto a unicorn, lifting Phoebe up before her. Then, with a triumphant whoop he jumped onto his own mount's back, and the two unicorns streaked off towards the forest, carrying the children with them.

22

The Quarry

It was not for nothing that Sadie had spent every afternoon for a year in Cap'n Ichabod's stable. She loved to ride, and she rode well, even under those outrageous conditions. She urged the unicorn on gently with her heels, and she leaned over its neck, pushing Phoebe down so they were part of the streamlined animal. The forest was before them, like a green sanctuary where the Dragons could not fly, and they were almost to its safety.

"Don't worry," Picker called, wincing a little as he slipped again on the unicorn's bare back. "The Lalawani can't catch us—they made the mistake of putting *me* in charge of the unicorns. I remembered how you said that Dragon blood let you talk to animals, so I told the unicorns I would let them all go if two of them would help us. The others all ran back to the meadows. Come on, Sadie! Ride faster! We're almost there!"

Maybe so, Sadie thought as she bent over her sister, maybe so—but the Lalawani weren't the only ones who wanted to catch them. When she looked over her shoulder, the sky behind them was black with twirling Dragon bodies. But the smell of their sulfurous fire was all the unicorns needed to goad them on faster than ever. With a great shout of triumph, the children were in the trees.

It was terribly dark within the forest. Behind them, Sadie and Picker could hear the angry calls of the pursuing Dragons, but the canopy of the trees was too dense and thick for them to fly. Sadie could hear them fall behind, wheezing and panting. She thought she heard Lalawani voices, too, and wondered if in their mutual desire to slaughter Phoebe, the ancient enemies had found a common cause. She nudged the unicorn on, but it needed no encouragement. When a horse smells the barn, it runs on under its own desire, and the unicorns smelled their barn now: the meadows of moongrass and starflowers where they had lived since time began. They hurried on, one long line from leveled horn to flapping tail, darting between the close-set trees, panting with exertion, and hunching up their backs to switch to a faster gait.

And then Sadie saw it: a deep ravine, a dark gash on the dark of the forest. There was no rein, nothing to turn the unicorn, but it wouldn't have mattered. The unicorn was running with the intoxicating pleasure of freedom, and it wanted to leap. It pulled itself together for the final sprint, readied itself for the jump, and then they were flying over the gully.

It wasn't supposed to happen that way. The unicorn was supposed to jump, and Sadie and Phoebe were supposed to sail over the ravine to a pause in the movie sound track music, and then they were supposed to land with the triumphant sound of four hooves hitting the leaf meal, one-two, three-four. But that wasn't the way it happened. Phoebe slipped first, or maybe Sadie only thought she did, but in any case, she threw her arms around her sister to keep her from falling, lost her seat on the unicorn's wide and slippery back, and they fell together.

It seemed to take a long time to fall, and a long time to see the stark white body of the unicorn pass over them, its silvery hooves just missing Phoebe's face. They fell and fell for what seemed like forever, and landed with a shock in the cold and wet of the water. Picker's unicorn passed over, too, and Sadie called out to him. She had one flash of Picker's white and frightened face, and then he, too, was gone, and she was being pulled away in the wild rushing of the river, holding on to her sister in a desperate attempt to keep both their faces above the surface of the icy water. She heard the distant bugle of a unicorn, and thought she heard the crackle of fire in the distance, but it was all a confused impression as the river bore them away.

There was no time to think of anything except trying to

breathe. In the hurly-burly kaleidoscope of the swirling river, the only constant thought in Sadie's head was that she refused to let Phoebe drown. "Keep your head up!" she ordered her sister, furious with fear, and then they were being spun around in the whirling of that water, banging painfully into sticks and rocks.

And then, suddenly, they had the uncomfortable good luck to smack into a log that lay across the river's path. Winded and bruised, but grateful, Sadie pushed Phoebe onto the trunk and hauled herself up, breathing heavily and closing her eyes in relief. The sisters sat there for a long time, not talking, and then Phoebe said, "I think the Dragons caught the unicorns."

Sadie thought of Picker with a spasm of nausea, and found she couldn't answer. But Phoebe understood her fear, and put her hand into her sister's and squeezed.

"Don't worry," she comforted Sadie in her wise little voice. "Picker doesn't ride very well. He probably fell off before they caught him."

Sadie sniffed. She had no time to worry about Picker, anyway. The river had swept them far away from their enemies, but she knew that when the Dragons got to the river, there would be no doubt which direction the current had carried them.

"Come on," she said to her sister. "We better go."

They walked a long time in those woods. They walked until the last light was gone from between the trees, and then they stumbled around in the dark. Often, Sadie wondered if they should not just sit and wait. You were supposed to stay still and wait, she knew, when you were lost, but that was only true when you wanted to be found. They kept going.

As the night wore on, Sadie marveled at how easily Phoebe tramped over the ground with her short stout legs, but then she realized that the Dragon blood that had helped her since the night Mrs. Fitz Edna died coursed even more strongly in Phoebe's veins. She peered through the dark then towards Phoebe.

"Aren't you even scared?" she asked.

"I was scared in the tower," Phoebe said simply. "But then you came."

This was decidedly gratifying to hear, but still Sadie herself was very scared. Her heart quickened like a rabbit's at every crackling twig. She felt hunted—in point of fact, she *was* hunted. There was a word for a hunted animal: *quarry,* and that's what she and Phoebe were. They were the *quarry,* and the Dragons and the Lalawani were the hunters, and Sadie did not at all like to think about what would happen if they were caught. Her heart hammered so hard she would not have been surprised if it beat a hole in her chest and jumped right out, to lie pulsing and twitching on the ground.

At last she couldn't stand it anymore.

"Come on," she whispered to Phoebe. "Let's stop for the night. Let's hide here."

Curled up with her sister on the roots of an enormous tree,

Sadie contemplated their future. Hiding; that's what they would do. They would become creatures of the night, slipping out for food and water when darkness covered them. That would be their dreary life, the life of a rabbit. She thought of home, and parents, and the carefree fun of not being hunted, and thought if only they could make it home, she would never take her life for granted again. She felt cold, and hungry, and miserable, and then she worried that the Dragon blood that had protected her for so long might be becoming diluted in her veins. She strained her ears to determine if she could hear the chatter of the night birds, to see if she could still understand what animals were saying, but they were too far away, and she wasn't sure. Then, in that night of horrible thoughts, she had another: what if her Dragon blood disappeared, and she could no longer understand the Dragons and the Lalawani? What if she stood before them with no way to plead for her life, to plead for either of their lives? She would be like a dumb animal, a hunted animal, a silent rabbit, the dumb quarry, and the thought of it made her sick to her stomach.

They slept then, Sadie fitfully, and Phoebe with the deluded confidence that she was finally safe, and in the morning, Sadie crept out to see what she could find to eat. She found a bush covered with berries and was just trying to decide if they were poisonous or not when she heard footsteps behind her. Her heart jumped into her throat, and she spun around to face her enemy. It was Phoebe.

"What are doing?" Sadie sputtered. "Are you *trying* to give me a heart attack?"

"I'm coming to help."

"You can help me by staying safe. I told you to stay in the tree. . . ." She stopped then. Her nervous ears had heard something, but that was not the worst. There was the unmistakable stench of sulfur and lizard, and that was how she knew they'd been caught. Her heart seemed to stop for a moment, and she closed her eyes in despair. She reached out to grab Phoebe's hand, and the sisters stood there, stock-still and terrified, as the Dragon moved into the grainy morning light.

He was not alone, either. Two Lalawani were with him, both still and resolute, mutilated by battle: one had a tattered wing that hung limply on its back, and the other had no wings at all. Sadie thought of how the Dragons treated their prisoners, and how the Lalawani treated theirs, and she was swept with cold fear. Instinctively, she moved in front of Phoebe. *How can you hurt her?* she screamed out, impotently, in her head. *How can you touch her, you, you—Barbazion?*

The three figures took a step forward then, and Sadie braced herself for the blow. Then one of the Barbazion spoke.

"It's them," it said in a tired voice, and Sadie raised her terrified eyes.

"Arananu?" she guessed.

A cowboy's yodel answered her, and Picker threw himself on her neck. "I can't *believe* we found you!" he shouted.

Beside him, the Dragon let out a great sulfurous sigh. "It is a miracle, Sadie-Human," he said, shaking his heavy head. "When I saw your beast without a rider, I was mostly certain you would be dead. But then the Picker-Human reminded me that if I was only *mostly* certain, than I must be a little *un*certain. So we looked for you, and here you are."

"Oh, Xpql!" Sadie cried, rushing to him.

"That's enough of that," the Dragon said in his gruff voice. "We still may not have time to do all we need to do. Others are still looking, and if *we* can find you, then they . . ." He let out a morose puff of smoke to finish his sentence.

"But what are we going to do?" Sadie asked, bewildered.

"Find the way home, of course," Picker answered. "Arananu and Xpql will help us back."

"But the Portal . . ."

"Not through the Portal," explained Picker. "We're near the cave where I came out of the quarry—*that's* how we'll get back."

"The quarry?" Sadie asked, wrinkling her brow. "But you said the tunnel was full of water—how . . . ?"

"What did Mrs. Fitz Edna always say?" Picker asked, almost leaping from foot to foot in his excitement. "Where there's a will, there's a way—that's what she said."

"She also said not to swim in caves," Sadie objected.

But Picker didn't hear; he was already helping Phoebe onto Xpql's back.

"I don't understand," Sadie said, following behind them. She looked from Xpql to Arananu and addressed them both. "I thought you wanted to kill her," she whispered.

Xpql shot her an offended look. "She is the Princess," he said, "May Fire and Water Protect Her. And she is my sister, as I have told you many times before, and our grandmother would want her sent where she will be safe."

"And you?" Sadie asked Arananu.

The Lalawani stared at her through his blackened eyes. "Victory for my People seems impossible now," he said. "We have failed. Now we can only serve the Protector by protecting that which was given to us. And that is why I will help send you back to the place from where you came. It is my responsibility, because I was the one who risked your life for our glory. And I owe it to Hanaloni, too. I lied to her, Sadu. She did not forgive me for it—she died asking after you, asking after a stranger whom she called close-to-daughter. So I do this for Hanaloni, and for you, Sadu, for you, too, Pickelu, for you stood by me in my captivity. But most of all, I do it for my Protector."

They walked on in silence. The only sound was the Xpql's wheezing as he plodded along in his slow lizard's gait. Then Picker said, "It's over here."

It was a little pool at the edge of the forest, near a broad field. Xpql stood still and waited for Phoebe to climb off his back, and the five of them stood staring down into the black water.

"But how . . ." Sadie started. She turned to Picker. "How far is it? Can we swim through?"

Picker shook his head. "I don't think so," he said. "The only reason I made it before was that the water was rushing so fast it pushed me through the tunnel. Otherwise, I would have drowned."

"I can do it," Phoebe volunteered.

"What are you talking about?" Sadie asked her. "You can't even swim!"

"I can, too." Phoebe sulked. "I always swim in Dragon-land. We go swimming in the unicorn meadow and the grandfather unicorn made me a swing out of flowers."

"She *is* one of the People," Xpql agreed. "We can go for long minutes without breathing."

"I can't let you do it," Sadie said. "I'm responsible. . . ."

But Phoebe had already jumped in, and the waters closed over her head. Sadie called out, and almost leapt after her, but suddenly there was a gurgle and a flushing sound, and the water drained out of the pool, leaving a tunnel into the darkness. Then Phoebe's face reappeared.

"It's all right," she said happily. "I pushed my hands through the thick part, and all the water went back. I put the water back into the quarry."

Sadie stared at her. "Why didn't tell me you could swim, back when we were in the river? I practically *killed* myself, trying to keep your head up above the water!"

She turned back to the others. Picker was gripping Ara-nanu's hand and Xpql's shoulder and staring at them both intently.

"We have to go," he was saying. "But *thank* you. And good luck. I hope that the fighting will be over now, and I hope neither of you will get in trouble for this."

"I may well be punished for what I do today," Arananu said. The look of proud resignation was back on his face, as it had been when he had stepped into the circle of the Dragons in the forest. "And I deserve punishment for failing the Protector. But perhaps we will salvage something from my mistakes. Perhaps we will settle for peace, since we cannot have victory."

Xpql nodded. "We have discussed this with the Picker-Human, my sister. We will bring our leaders back here and ask the Barbazion to bring their Rock-Breaker. We will seal this entrance shut, with witnesses, and then my People and the Barbazion will know that the Princess is gone and victory will never be certain. Perhaps we can go back to the way it was before, with the small battles and skirmishes. As for me, they can do with me as they wish for my part in letting the Princess escape. And as you once said yourself, Sadie-Human, 'It is better to die closer to your goal, for then you feel you have accomplished something.'"

"But maybe no one will be angry, Xpql!" Sadie said excitedly. "Maybe they won't even have skirmishes anymore. Maybe you can all see that peace with your enemies *is* victory. The Prophecy about the golden egg child could really be true, after all. Maybe Phoebe can bring victory to both sides, by bringing peace to your planet."

She turned to Xpql and Arananu and beamed at both of them. "There really *could* be a time of everlasting light, just like the Prophecy said. When your People see that the two of you have become friends . . ."

Xpql and Arananu each took a step away from the other at that. "We are not *friends*," Arananu stressed. "I do this for you children, for the reasons I have said. No one will ever accuse me of being *friends* with the Barbazion."

"Nor I," Xpql stressed with a hot rush of air. "The memory of what was done to Xthltg and to Skpbl will be with me always. I do this for you and the Princess, Sadie-Human. I owe nothing to the Barbazion." He stared at Arananu with disgust at the very idea of friendship with the enemy.

"But—" Sadie protested. "Please, Xpql! Please, Arananu! I love you both—that should show you that neither of you is bad!"

"If you love me, go now," begged Arananu, looking nervously over his shoulder at the exposed plains behind them. "Let me know you are safe before the others come."

Xpql pressed his hand against his chest. "My fire pains me," he said. "It is worse when I worry. *Please* go, Sadie-Human. I want to know you are safe, too. My grandmother always spoke highly of you. I believe she was right."

"Let's *go*," said Phoebe impatiently. "I want to see Mama and Daddy! Come, Sadie! Make her come, Picker!"

Sadie looked at Arananu, and at Xpql, and back at the misty fields of Dragonland. She could think of nothing else to say. Instead, she waved awkwardly and climbed down into the tunnel after Phoebe. Picker followed at her heels.

The walls of the tunnel still glistened with water, but there was something familiar about them, as if they were Earth rocks and not the rocks of Dragonland. And then, at the end of the tunnel, Sadie saw a familiar sight: the gray-green water of the quarry, the rays of sunlight reaching down through it.

The three of them stood there a moment, looking at the wall of water, and Phoebe eagerly reached out her hand. But Sadie glanced back at the distant light that shone on Dragonland and felt a hollow ache she knew nothing would ever entirely fill.

"Wait," she said suddenly. She raced back up the tunnel to where Arananu and Xpql stood guard.

"Be safe," she said to their surprised faces, and then, with a little wave, she ran back down the tunnel towards Picker and Phoebe, and home.